HARD TIME

Debt Collector 8

JON MILLS

DIRECT RESPONSE PUBLISHING

ISBN-13: 978-1544913988
ISBN-10: 1544913982

Dedication

For my family.

Prologue - Blind Man

YOSEMITE NATIONAL PARK

Jack Winchester finished taping the man's hands to the dashboard and his feet to the underside of the seat of the brand-new Audi Allroad. After, he gave him a pat on the cheek.

"There we go. Can't be too safe."

Devin frowned, an expression of terror on his face. "Who the hell are you, man?"

"Doesn't matter."

He stuttered. "What, what… what are you doing?"

"What does it look like? We're going for a drive. You know, I've always wanted to take out one of these all-road vehicles and just look around." He waved his arms towards the breathtaking view of the Rocky Mountains, and the valley full of lush forest. "Can you get a better place than this?"

"What about my seat belt?"

"You're already strapped in."

Jack slammed the passenger door before he could say another word and strolled around to the trunk, popped it open and took out a bottle of bourbon from a grocery bag. He glanced at it for a second, turning it in his hand. He squinted as a hard noonday sun reflected off the bottle. *Wild Turkey Bourbon 101?* He'd heard good things about it.

Jack slammed the trunk and slipped into the driver's side. He breathed in relishing every second. Devin McCabe glanced at him. He twisted off the cap and took a swig. Jack winced and spat it out all over the console in front of him. "Shit! That is nasty."

He shuddered.

"C'mon, man, what the hell is this about?"

"For someone that likes the finer things in life, Devin,

your choice in beverages strikes me as a little odd. Like, couldn't you have picked up something better?"

"I like Wild Turkey. Look man, who gives a fuck. Who put you up to this? Is this a prank?"

Jack took another swig then tossed it in the back. "Oh, it's not a prank, that is for sure."

"Then what are we doing?"

Jack took out a cigarette and lit it. He gazed out across Yosemite National Park as he blew out gray smoke. They were high in the mountains and were idling at the edge of a narrow and treacherous winding pass called Tioga Road.

"Open your ears. I told you. Are you mentally challenged?"

He smirked at Devin and waited to see if he would understand what Jack was getting at. Only two hours before, he had abducted him from a small town in Mono County.

Devin shook his head. "You are out of your mind."

"All the best ones are. Now just sit back and enjoy the ride." Jack brought the window down and breathed in the crisp mountain air. He narrowed his eyes and stifled a laugh. "Do you want some music on?"

He didn't wait for him to reply. A quick press and twist of a button, and they tuned into some country music. Jack leaned back in his seat and got comfy. Several cars shot by oblivious to what was taking place behind the dark tinted windows.

"Thirty-nine miles long, almost ten thousand feet above sea level, it offers some of the most beautiful views of Yosemite — pity I won't get to see any," Jack muttered.

Devin jerked his head to the left.

"What?"

Jack fished out of his leather jacket pocket a piece of black cloth. He wrapped it around his eyes and tied it off at the back of his head.

"What are you doing?"

"Oh don't worry, you'll be my eyes." He sniffed hard, then took another puff of his cigarette before tossing it out the window. A hard wind blew it away as a large truck came flying past them.

"Now remember, I can't see shit, so I'm dependent upon you."

Devin snorted. "You are fucking loco. Let me out of here."

What he didn't know was Jack could see through the thin material. It wasn't clear but he could make out shapes and the edge of the road — Devin didn't know.

"Please, man. We can work this out, just let me go." He struggled but it was pointless. The duct tape was so tight it was almost cutting off his circulation.

Jack tapped the steering wheel.

"Right, let's get this show on the road, shall we? Or maybe I should say, off the road as I'm not too sure how long we'll be on the road."

He turned over the ignition and the car growled to life. "Oh, just listen to that engine purr, she can't wait to get started. Damn, this is exciting."

Jack hit the gas and they lunged forward and then he slammed his foot on the brake.

"False start, I needed to make sure I knew where the brake was."

He could hear Devin's breathing getting rapid, he was swallowing hard and panic was taking over. "Listen, just tell me, what it is you want?"

"I want nothing. Well, that's a lie, I want answers and you will give them or... we'll see how we do on this narrow stretch of road."

Jack took a recorder out of his pocket and placed it on the dashboard. "Tell me the truth about Bobby Dumar."

"Who?"

Jack hit the gas, then slammed his foot on the brake causing Devin to bang his head on the glass. Jack had positioned him in such a way that he was leaning forward.

Devin let out a groan. "Fuck. I don't know what you—"

"Wrong answer."

Jack hit the gas and this time they tore away. He pulled out onto the road and drove erratically as if he couldn't see where he was going. A vehicle rushed by them and honked its horn as they came within spitting distance of it.

"Pull over. Pull over!" Devin shouted.

"Which way? Left?" He swerved into the oncoming lane. Jack knew what Devin meant but he acted ignorant. With the way the road curved around the mountain, at any second a vehicle could come rushing around the bend and it would be over. Well, at least one vehicle would have gone over. Large sections of the winding road had no barrier, the only areas that had them were on the sharp curves so Jack exaggerated his inability to see by getting as close as he could to the edge while attempting to avoid oncoming traffic. The screams coming from Devin were priceless. God, he was having a hoot, scaring the shit out of this guy.

"Go right," Devin screamed as a truck came around the bend. They missed it by inches.

"Come on, Devin."

"I told you. I don't know. Look man, surely you don't want to die?"

"I don't care, Devin."

"Everyone cares."

"Not me," Jack replied.

He swerved the vehicle all over the road, getting dangerously close to the edge each time. Seconds felt like minutes as Jack waited for him to confess. He continued the cycle of swerving until Devin couldn't handle it anymore.

"All right, all right, I'll tell you what you want to know, just take the damn cover off your eyes."

Jack whipped it off and pulled over to another pit stop. He chuckled to himself as he turned to find Devin sweating.

"How was the view?" Jack asked patting him on the back. "So?" Jack said picking up the recorder.

"I killed her. It was me, okay. But it was an accident."

"An accident? If it was an accident, then why did you let Bobby take the fall?"

"Because he was mentally challenged and he was known for being too friendly with her. Everyone had seen him pestering her."

"And yet you knew that was just his way. He had no intentions of harming her, did he?"

"No but I was scared."

"Scared of admitting it was an accident?" Jack asked.

"Scared of going to jail. Scared of losing my business. Scared of what my wife would think of me."

Jack snorted and then sighed. "At no point in any of that did I hear you mention Bobby or his mother."

"Look does it matter? It's done now." He exhaled hard. "He's behind bars, they classed it as manslaughter, first offense. He'll be out in five years with good behavior."

Jack sank back in his seat. "Well that makes me feel so much better. Damn, I wish you had told me earlier. This could have all been avoided." Jack paused. He was messing with him. "But that's the problem, Devin. That's five years too many, so here's what you will do. You will record your confession, lead me to where the weapon is that you used to kill her, and then I will hand your ass in."

His eyes flared and he slowly shook his head. "I can't do that. No, I'll do anything else but that. It will ruin my family. Our business. Everything."

"It already has. Except it's ruined someone else's life. Time to man up and put things right."

"No. I'll give you money. Anything you want, but I can't do that."

Jack let out a heavy sigh and wrapped the black band back around his eyes.

"Oh, come on man. Cut me a break. They can't be paying enough that you would be willing to die."

Jack scoffed. "I don't need the incentive of money to want to die."

He started the vehicle up and began to veer out into what would have been traffic when Devin shouted, "Okay! Enough. I will do it. I'll say whatever the hell you want me to say."

Jack killed the engine. "I don't want you to say anything. Bobby's mother does."

Devin sank his head against the dashboard as Jack put the digital recorder near his face. "State your name, age, where you are from, what happened, the time it happened, how you killed her, where the weapon is now, and that Bobby Dumar had nothing to do with it."

Devin glanced at it. For a few seconds, he hesitated and then he began his confession.

After they collected a knife he'd buried in a forest not far from his home, Jack drove him to the nearest sheriff's office. Now he could have taken him inside and handed him over to the cops but that would have raised too many questions. Vigilante justice was frowned upon, as was abduction and scaring the shit out of a guy on a mountain.

So, when he arrived he took Devin out of the vehicle and duct-taped the digital recorder and a message on a piece of paper to the front of his chest, along with the knife that had murdered the girl. He marched him up to the door, turned on the recorder and pushed him inside. Before he did, he had one last thing to say.

"If it comes to my attention you have attempted to twist, or wiggle your way out of this in any form, I will return and this time that trip on the road will feel like a kid's ride at a fair compared to the next one I'll take you on. You understand?"

A despondent and tearful-looking Devin shuffled into the station, his hands still bound, though this time behind his back.

The message on the front of his chest would explain.

The digital recording would have his confession.

And the knife had his prints and her DNA.

As Jack walked away he never phoned Bobby's mother to arrange delivery of payment, she had suffered enough and he didn't need the money.

This job, he did just to get his mind off the past.

One - Old Friends

His head jerked forward as the Greyhound bus driver applied the brakes. Jack's eyes blinked awake. His mouth was dry and he could feel a tension headache at the back of his skull. It was stifling hot because the air conditioning had given up the ghost a few miles back. Even with the windows cracked, a blazing sun beat through the glass making him feel nauseated. He gazed around at the other travelers and reached into his jacket pocket for the stainless steel hip flask. He flipped the lid and took a hard swig. The bourbon burned the back of his throat but soothed a parched mouth. Passengers shuffled down the narrow walkway to exit the bus. He waited until it was almost empty before squeezing out and grabbing his backpack. There wasn't much inside: a few toiletries, some cash, a bottle of water, a dog-eared secondhand copy of *On the Road* by Jack Kerouac and a map of the United States. He rolled his head around to work out the kinks. It had been three months since the death of Isabel. After selling off his Florida property at a ridiculously low price, he spent a little time in Texas, holed up in a motel close to a dingy bar. His days didn't begin before noon and they usually ended one of three ways — passed out in some alley, tossed out of some taxi or tangled up with some woman.

The following month wasn't much better, he buried himself in back-to-back jobs, doing anything to keep his mind occupied, even at the risk of his safety, health and sanity. It didn't matter how much clients wanted to pay, or even how dangerous the job was. Yes, was always his answer. Strange as it may have seemed, somewhere in those moments when he was beating on some loser who had knocked a woman around, or ducked out of paying child support, he found peace. Of course it didn't last. It never did. The second he closed the door at the motel, his mind would churn over the past and all the what-ifs. As hard as he tried to occupy his mind, he couldn't escape the memories.

There'd been a few times in a drunken state he'd placed the barrel of his gun against his temple and contemplated pulling the trigger. It would have been all over. No more pain. No more regrets. No more struggling to stay positive.

And yet every time, he couldn't bring himself to do it.

Like an angel sitting on his shoulder, whispering in his ear, he knew deep down it wasn't the answer.

But the problem was, neither was a bottle of bourbon, overworking or sex every night.

It only numbed him for a while. It was short-lived satisfaction and then he was back to square one — listening to his thoughts.

Somewhere in the third month he got the phone call from John Dalton. Call it fate or an angel on his shoulder but it was exactly what he needed. He just didn't know it at the time.

They touched base every couple of months but in all that had occurred, he'd forgotten to call him. Of course, Dalton was surprised. It was usually Jack annoying him with late-night phone calls. Most of the time it was just shooting the breeze but it eventually circled back around to what he was doing with his life. Somewhere in Dalton's mind he was determined to save Jack.

From what? It was anyone's guess. Jack was just glad to have someone to unload his problems on.

Words were exchanged, an invitation was given and here he was — back in Los Angeles, the land of sunshine, palm trees and broken dreams.

Jack thanked the bus driver as he exited. He squinted and raised a forearm to block the glare of the sun. Outside, passengers collected their baggage, some transferred to idling taxis while others went into the station on Seventh Street. A Greyhound bus honked its horn as it edged its way out onto the main street. The smell of fast food wafted over from a hotdog vendor. His stomach grumbled. Jack donned a pair of dark sunglasses, pushed his baseball cap down and began the short walk to 54 South San Pedro Street.

Not much had changed.

Skid Row was still the hellish nightmare he remembered. An endless array of psych patients, crack addicts, heroin users, gang members, artists and vets shielding themselves from the elements and the world's eyes in tents and cardboard boxes pressed up against walls. Despised by society, overlooked by the government, they were the throwaways. And yet right now, he felt more at home among them than ever before.

When he entered the doors of the Unified Rescue Mission he smiled. Across the room, among the many faces of the addicted, homeless and hungry was Dalton. A short, stocky man with light hair and dark eyes, he still looked the same. He was having a heated exchange with a dark-skinned man and a woman disgruntled about something. Both of them looked like vagrants. Shabby clothes, matted hair and dust-covered skin. Jack observed for a few minutes wondering at what point Dalton would notice him.

"Raymond, do you remember what I told you?"

"Oh come on, he provoked me."

"This is not the place to unleash your anger."

"She said he touched her."

"And you have my word, I will look into it."

"I'm not leaving until you do."

He shook his head. "Look, take a seat and I will go speak with him now but I can't guarantee anything."

"Well if you can't, I can."

The wide, heavyset man went to push past him and Dalton put his hand out. Obviously the wrong thing to do as this guy was in a foul mood. He slapped Dalton's hand out of the way and shoved him back into a set of folding chairs. They crumpled beneath him. He was just about to throw a punch when Jack grabbed his wrist.

"What the fuck?"

Before he knew what was happening, Jack twisted it around and shoved it up hard. Meanwhile the woman had got in on the action and had jumped on top of Jack's back. After a short scuffle, some string bean hired security guard came over to lend a hand and they were soon tossed out and told not to come back until they could behave.

Jack stood at the main entrance with the guard.

"Thanks for helping."

"Not a problem," Jack replied.

Behind him he could hear John Dalton muttering something to two women about how things would be okay, and not to worry. As soon as Jack turned, a smile spread across his face.

Dalton exhaled hard. "I should have figured. Every time the shit hits the fan, you seem to be in the general vicinity. You're like a magnet for trouble."

He came over and they both hugged it out.

"Good to see you, Jack."

"Likewise. I see you haven't lost your charm with the locals."

Dalton looked out the window, wiped a hand across his sweaty brow and sighed. "Yeah, these folks just don't seem to get the gist of how things function around here."

"And I see you have a new guard."

He rolled his eyes and motioned for Jack to follow him out back.

"He does a fine job of guarding the coffee machine but a poor job of dealing with high-strung addicts. You don't need a job, do you?"

He chuckled as he led him down the corridor to his office.

"So what was that all about?"

"Raymond checked in with his girlfriend a month ago. He thinks one of our volunteers got a little too friendly but it's just a misunderstanding. Whenever we are dealing with a woman, there is always a male and a female volunteer present. We nipped those sexual accusation issues in the bud a long time ago. No, he was just looking for a way to blow off steam because he'd been caught trying to sell crack to a few guys inside who were trying to kick the habit."

"Helpful."

"Exactly," Dalton said motioning for him to enter his office.

"Been a while since I was here."

"That it has. What's up with the beard? You going all

Grizzly Adams on me?"

Jack ran a hand across his face. He'd let himself go. Motivation wasn't exactly at the top of his list. "Thinking of trying a new look."

"And a new smell?"

Jack sniffed his armpits.

"I had a shower this morning," Jack protested.

Dalton smiled as he went around to his coffee machine and filled a filter with coffee grounds.

"I wasn't meaning your body odor. How long have you been drinking?"

Jack leaned back in a seat. "I didn't come all this way to be psychoanalyzed, John."

Dalton looked at him and raised his eyebrows but said nothing for a short while. He returned with two cups of coffee. "You still take it black?"

"Yeah."

He eased into his chair.

"You can't bullshit an ex-alcoholic, Jack."

"I don't have—"

"A problem with drink?" Dalton chuckled and sipped at his coffee. "That was my favorite line." He put his coffee down and studied Jack. "So how long has it been?"

"No offense, John, but I really don't want to get into it. You said you had a message for me?"

Dalton regarded him the way he did with anyone that sat across from him. There was kindness in his eyes and yet he wasn't the kind of man you could hide addiction from. Jack didn't think he had an addiction to alcohol. Sure, he had been drunk a little more since losing Isabel but that was normal. Wasn't it? At first he did it to numb the pain at night. Nights were the hardest. When he was lying on his bed, his mind wandered all over the place. A nice glass of bourbon quieted it. Nights soon turned into days and before he knew it he was feeling lost if he didn't have his steel flask inside his jacket.

Dalton reached into his desk and pulled out a scrap of paper. He made a quick phone call.

"Yeah, he's here. Ten minutes? Sure. You want to speak to him?"

He nodded and then hung up.

"I hope that wasn't the cops."

Dalton chuckled. "Honestly, Jack, you'd think you would know me by now."

He cocked his head to one side. The truth was he trusted no one. Perhaps it was the alcohol making him paranoid, or just the lingering thought in the back of his mind that one day the FBI would come knocking again. He still didn't know why they had let him go, though Agent Cooper seemed adamant that they would not be looking for him.

"How come you couldn't just give me the message over the phone?"

"Because she wanted to speak to you in person."

Jack frowned. "She?"

"You'll see. She'll be here soon. In the meantime, what's going on with yourself? No phone call for months. It's not like you, Jack."

Jack hadn't told him what had taken place in Florida or how close he had got to Isabel or how much her death had affected him. He wasn't one for bringing others down, especially not Dalton. He had enough on his plate. Every day the mission was dealing with situations that were far worse than his. It felt absurd to even mention his troubles. No, he kept them close to his chest. The only time he let them slip past his lips was after several drinks. And the only ones that heard them were bartenders. People who would forget the second they clocked out from their shift.

Trying to duck out of the conversation, Jack picked up a photo of Dalton and his family.

"How's Karen doing? I see the baby is getting big."

Dalton leaned over and took it from him.

"Answer the question."

Jack smirked before he pursed his lips. "What do you want to hear, John? That everything has turned out the way I hoped it would? That you were right? That maybe I should have listened to what Eddie said about staying clear of anyone I cared about? Cause I've gone both ways and it doesn't matter what I do, people end up dead because of me." He paused. "But I guess that's the stuff you thrive on, isn't it? The hard cases? The ones that don't think they can be reached?"

Dalton sipped at his coffee. "Why do you keep looking back?"

"Because I see nothing up ahead."

Dalton rocked back and forth slowly in his chair. "So what? You going to lose yourself in a bottle now?"

"I lost myself a long time ago, John, and it wasn't in a bottle."

"Eddie told me about your upbringing." He sucked air between his teeth. "Not much you can do about what happened but you can choose how to move forward."

Jack shook his head. "I don't know about that."

"Why don't you stick around here? You know I could use someone like you."

"Use?"

Dalton shook his head. "Always thinking about how others are trying to take advantage of you." He breathed in deeply. "Ah, it's to be expected. No, I didn't mean it like that. No man's an island, Jack. Humanity might not agree on how they ended up on this ball of dirt, but one thing for sure is we aren't meant to live alone."

"I hope that's not what you pitch to those folks lining the streets outside because I think their lives tell a different story."

"You're right. The fact is, Jack, we are a product of our upbringing. We don't get to choose what family we enter, or who raises us, and those early years will shape who we become but that doesn't mean who we become is set in stone."

Jack waved his hand. "Please. Save it for the needy, Dalton."

Dalton leaned forward. "Everyone needs. The question is, what do you need, Jack?"

"A drink, and perhaps a warm female. You think you can hook me up?"

He stared at him. "What are you scared of?"

Jack shrugged and downed his coffee. There was a long pause as Dalton waited for his answer. Jack wasn't delaying answering, he just hadn't taken the time to think about it.

"If you must know. Everything I have loved, or has ever meant anything is gone."

"Not everyone," a female voice piped up from behind them. The door cracked open a little wider and Jack swiveled in his chair. As his eyes fell upon the aged woman, he squinted. She had to have been in her late sixties, early seventies. Graying hair, pulled back tight. A hard complexion as if weathered by time. She wore a pair of blue jeans, flip flops and a white V-neck shirt. There was something about her that was familiar and yet he couldn't determine what.

Dalton got up from his chair and made a waving motion, "Jack, this is—"

"Liz. Your mother."

Two Confession

Jack rose from his seat and stared at the woman before his eyes darted to Dalton's. None of this was making sense. John Dalton wasn't the kind of man to mess with his head. He knew everything he'd been through. He knew he was already teetering on the edge of an abyss, one which he might not recover from. What the hell was this all about?

"Is this some kind of joke?" Jack asked.

The woman claiming to be his mother stepped forward, her eyes soaking him in.

"You really have Eddie's eyes."

Jack took a few steps back as Liz put out a hand as if trying to explore his face.

"Right, this must be very confusing."

"Confusing? Dalton, you want to tell me what's going on here?"

Liz looked at Dalton as if waiting to see whether he

would clarify.

"Um, best you take a seat, Jack."

"I'll stand."

He spoke in a low tone and made his way back around to his desk, as if that would protect him from Jack's anger. "Okay, well—"

"John, let me explain," Liz said. "Here's the thing."

Jack shook his head. "No. No, you were meant to have died after giving birth to my sister."

"I know what people told you."

He frowned trying to grasp what was happening. "But the hospital, they said you went missing, while others said my father, well... not Eddie but you know... that he killed you."

She nodded. "I know this won't be easy to understand, Jack."

Jack had heard enough, his head was spinning. He moved towards the door and flung it open and headed out.

"Jack!" Dalton shouted out. Jack was already halfway

down the corridor when he caught up with him. He grabbed a hold of his bicep.

"Wait up. You need to hear her out."

Jack turned, glancing back towards Dalton's office where Liz was looking out.

"I don't need to listen to any of this. You knew about my past. Why on earth would you believe this woman?"

"I didn't, Jack. She showed me your birth certificate. Besides, you must recognize her from old photos?"

"I've only ever seen one photo of her and it was when she was young."

"Your father never kept any?"

"Which one?"

It was confusing. On one hand, he'd grown up believing the man he lived with was his father, and then on the other he had the confession from Eddie Carmine in the form of a letter. So many secrets. So many lies. At this age, he no longer cared.

"You know what I mean," Dalton said.

Jack chuckled and shook his head.

"Give her a chance to explain."

Jack shot a sideways glance up the corridor. While he found the whole thing absurd, he couldn't help be curious. Though he'd been told that she'd died in childbirth, rumor was his father had killed her. When Jack asked around, others in the neighborhood said she went missing. Even Eddie confirmed that.

"Listen, I'll knock off early and we can all go back to my place. I'll have Karen put together a lunch and you can hear what she has to say. If you still think it's bullshit, then I apologize but—"

"When did she show up?" Jack asked, cutting him off.

Dalton swallowed hard and looked down at his feet.

"When?" Jack asked in a more demanding tone.

"Three weeks ago. I tried phoning but you weren't answering your messages."

"Why is she here?"

"I think it's best she explains that."

Jack ground his teeth. This was the last thing he wanted. His life was complex enough as it was without this bombshell. Jack shifted his weight from one foot to the next and scratched his beard. He looked back at the woman claiming to be his mother. He'd never bonded with her. He felt nothing. He could have walked out the door and continued on his way without giving it a second thought but he was curious. If it was her, why was she showing up now? Jack gave a reluctant nod and Dalton patted him on the arm.

"Just give me five minutes to sort out things with my staff and we'll head out. Okay?"

He dashed off looking flustered leaving Jack standing at one end of the corridor while his mother was at the other end. To say it was awkward would be an understatement. He had a million and one questions and yet asking even one would have meant accepting her claim and right now he wasn't buying it. Instead his mind was going through a list of names. People who might have been trying to lure him out into the open. The Mafia. The FBI. Disgruntled clients. The families of those he had killed. He lived his life with his guard up. It had to be that way.

"John said you've turned your life around. Got away from the Mafia."

An eyebrow shot up. Was she expecting him to enter deep conversation about his life? When he didn't reply, she continued.

"Anyway, it's a good thing. I never thought Jersey was a good place to raise a family."

"Is that why you left us behind?"

She took a few steps forward and then her brow knit together. "I know this can't be easy, Jack. But I…"

Thankfully, before she could finish, Dalton reemerged and motioned for them to follow him out to the parking lot. They entered a black SUV; Jack hopped in the passenger side while Liz was in the back. Throughout the entire journey, he could feel her eyes boring into him. Dalton tried to keep the mood light by starting a dialogue with Liz but Jack could tell that it wasn't working. The tension in the air could have been cut with a knife.

When they arrived at Dalton's home, Karen looked as

if she had already been prepped for what was liable to become a very heated discussion. She greeted Jack with open arms though he could tell she wasn't comfortable having him there. The last time he'd been in his home, Dalton was treating him for bullet and knife wounds.

Karen led them into a dining area. She had already set out the table with some sushi, a few ham sandwiches and different finger foods. She excused herself and said she had a prior appointment. A likely story but Jack didn't mind. The fewer eyes on him the better.

"Please, take a seat," Dalton said, pulling out a chair. Liz eyed Jack and he waited until she had decided where she would sit before he sat across from her. After a few minutes of awkward silence, they helped themselves to food and then the questions rolled.

Three - Bombshell

He wanted answers and she would give them. He squinted at her from across the table as he piled vegetables onto his plate. Jack was looking for any similarities. Something that might indicate that she was his mother. But he couldn't see it. The photo he'd seen when he was a kid belonged to Eddie, he didn't keep it on him because like most things in his past, he preferred to forget.

"Do you have questions?" Liz kicked it off.

"Why should I believe you're my mother?"

She rifled through her purse and pulled out paperwork. From a small package she retrieved a birth certificate, and several photos. One inside the hospital after she had given birth, another outside as Jack could see a sign for the New Jersey hospital. The last was of her face black-and-blue from a beating. She then handed him a few pieces of her ID with her signature. They matched the one on the birth certificate. Her name, however, was

41

no longer Liz Winchester, she now went under the name Liz Matthews.

He nodded. All of it could have been forged. It wasn't like he hadn't worked with skilled individuals that could forge certificates and create fake IDs. Hell, after what he went through in New York, he'd considered having plastic surgery to make it easier to vanish but he never did.

He continued chewing.

"Questions?"

Jack snorted as he loaded his mouth with food. "Sure. Here's a question for you. Actually, here are three. If you are my mother, where were you when that asshole was beating on me? Or where were you when your daughter was abused and ended up in the East Star Behavioral Treatment Center? And where were you when Eddie was trying to figure out how to explain that he was my father?"

She set her knife and fork down and took a sip of her drink.

"I didn't know about that. I swear. Eddie never mentioned it."

Eddie never mentioned it?

She continued. "Listen, I know you're angry. You have every right. I would be. I don't expect you to understand or accept what I did back then, but you have to know, Jack, I was a very different person. Beatings were an everyday occurrence. I only had two options. Kill him or leave him. I knew if I left with you both he would have found me, so Eddie helped me to leave. He said he would watch out for you both."

Jack leaned back in his seat and frowned. Eddie hadn't told him that. He studied her face looking for cracks in her demeanor but there were none.

"Eddie knew all along?"

She nodded.

"He knew where you were?"

"There wasn't a day that went by I didn't think about you or your sister."

Jack snorted. "Ah, isn't that lovely. Well your good

thoughts went to waste because they didn't do us any good." Jack shoved his plate away. He'd just lost his appetite. "And as for watching over us. Yeah, Eddie did that but not even he could be there for every beating."

"Jack, I'm sorry. I know it doesn't mean much coming from me now but…"

Jack could feel his blood boiling inside him. He was used to dealing with difficult situations but this… this was right off the deep end. Liz nodded and attempted to reach over and touch his hand. Jack pulled it back. "Don't."

She pulled her hand away and continued to eat.

"How about you start by telling me where the hell you've been all these years and why after all this time you have decided to show your face." Jack cast a fiery glance at Dalton. "Or let me guess, you've found God and this is some means of making amends?"

"Jack," Dalton interjected.

"You've got a brother, Jack," Liz blurted out.

He looked at her and a smile danced on his lips. "Well

isn't that something. I assume he wasn't just born yesterday by the looks of you. So do tell. Why did you feel the need to tell me now? Or did my brother talk you into it?"

"Actually, he did. Somewhat."

Jack shook his head. "I figured you wouldn't have been here of your own volition."

"It's not like that."

"No? Then how is it?"

She glanced at Dalton and Jack followed her gaze. "Why do I get the sense you have known each other longer than three weeks?"

Dalton put his drink down, pursed his lips and answered him. "I've known Liz for over fourteen years."

Jack ran a hand over his face. The revelations just kept coming. "Oh, now how about that. More secrets. More lies. And you call yourself a minister?"

"I'm not exactly a minister."

"But you sell people on God, do you not?"

"It's part of my job. I never created the program at the

45

mission."

Jack put his fork down and contemplated leaving. He was tired of listening to lies.

"If it's any consolation, John didn't know I was your mother until recently."

"How recent?"

She paused before replying, "A year ago."

Jack snorted and picked at the tablecloth.

"I saw the news about Sheng Ping, and several other details that mentioned your name in the paper."

Dalton interjected. "She came by, asking a lot of questions. I said nothing, Jack, but when she showed me," he motioned to the package in front of him. "Well, she asked me to not say anything to you."

He nodded unsure of what to believe.

"So does my brother have a name?"

"Noah."

"How old?"

"Thirty-eight."

She reached into her purse and pulled out a crinkled

photo. She slipped it across the table. It was a photo of Liz and another man, a man that looked very similar to Jack in the face. Whereas Jack was six foot, muscular and had a thick head of hair, Noah had the height but not the build. He was thin as if he had neglected his body. He didn't look unhealthy but he also didn't look like he had a gym membership.

"And where is he?"

She hesitated before replying. "Honduras. Noah is in prison, Jack."

Jack rubbed the bridge of his nose and stifled a laugh. He couldn't help find that amusing. "Good to see he's following in his brother's footsteps."

She didn't look as if she found it funny.

"And?"

"Noah was on a missions trip."

He chuckled. "A missions trip? Okay, scratch the part about following in my footsteps."

Dalton rolled his eyes and took a hard chug on his bottle of beer. There was silence for a minute or two as if everyone was contemplating what to say next.

"Anyway, he went down there with a group of friends and hooked up with some missions organization trying to make a difference."

Jack interrupted. "Make a difference. Man, has that line led people down the wrong road. But please go ahead."

Liz looked at Dalton as if trying to get guidance for whether to continue. He motioned to her and then glared at Jack.

"Anyway, he was meant to return over three weeks ago."

"Ah, hence the reason you got in contact three weeks ago." He motioned with a nod to Dalton. "So you weren't lying," Jack said with a smirk forming at the corner of his mouth. "Continue."

"They have him in on some charge of attempting to leave Honduras with cocaine."

Jack stifled a laugh. "And you don't think your boy loves to snort a little, right?"

"Jack," Dalton said in a manner that a close friend might if someone had overstepped the line.

"Don't Jack me. What the hell has that got to do with me? We all make choices. Hell, I've made some real doozies. In fact, I could tell you a few stories that would add more gray hairs to your head."

"They're going to kill him."

"What, for drug trafficking? Come on. He'll be out in no time with a good lawyer. And that can be sped up by flashing some green. I'm sure you have money stashed away, right?"

Both of them looked at him.

"What? You want me to bail him out? I mean I have money but not that much, and I don't think it's going cut it down there. The government is corrupt."

"I don't want you to bail him out. I want you to get him out."

Jack laughed, leaning back in his chair. "And how do you suppose I do that?"

There was silence between the two of them and then it

sank in.

Jack narrowed his eyes, and cleared his throat. "You want me to help him escape?"

Four - Gambler's Heart

Fifteen minutes later, Jack entered a hotel. He left them slack-jawed and staring out an open front door. After hearing what his mother had in mind, he didn't even let her finish the conversation. It was ludicrous. He upped and left without even thanking Dalton. He might be stupid enough to take on dangerous jobs for clients but breaking people out of prison was where he drew the line. The thought of going anywhere near a U.S. prison was enough to make him break out in a cold sweat but Danlí, the toughest prison in Honduras? That had him running for the hills.

No amount of money could convince him.

Nope, whatever his brother had got himself into, he would have to fix that shit himself. Dalton had tried to persuade him to stay at his home, but he needed his space. His mind was in overdrive and the last thing he wanted was to have him droning in his ear about families sticking together. Where was she when he needed her?

He planned on booking into the DoubleTree in the downtown. It was a short walk from Dalton's place. He could have stayed at any hotel but after his first visit he thought an upgrade was in order. The moment he entered the warm lobby, the staff on duty and guests stared at him as if he would steal or cause trouble.

"I need a room for the night."

The gentleman behind the desk eyed him over the rim of his glasses. "Let me check that for you, sir."

He tapped away on his keyboard then made a face.

"Um, I'm afraid we are all booked up. Sorry."

Jack shook his head. "Come on, you must have one room."

"I'm sorry, sir."

"Right, well, I'll just take a seat over here and wait until someone cancels or leaves."

Jack strolled towards an upscale restaurant. In the reception area, everything was gleaming. His eyes scanned the highly polished floors, granite counters and gold-trimmed luggage carts. No money had been spared.

"Um, sir, you can't go in there. Only guests."

Jack ignored him and entered the restaurant and made a beeline for the bar. A hot girl dressed in a waistcoat and white shirt was cleaning glasses when he approached.

"A double bourbon."

The concierge caught up with him. "Excuse me, sir. I will need you to vacate the premises."

"Why?"

"Because this is for guests only."

Jack took a seat on a bar stool and turned his back to him. "Well, I will be a guest, real soon."

He straightened himself, trying to appear bigger than he was. "Look, I don't want to call security."

"Security?" Jack turned and fished out a bunch of money. "How much do you need? Is this enough?" He tossed down four hundred-dollar bills. By the look on his face even the sight of money would not convince this guy. "What, my money not green enough?"

He caught sight of himself in the mirror behind the

JON MILLS

bottles of spirits. Sure, he looked as though he'd been dragged through a bush backwards. His hair was in a state, his beard out of control and he hadn't changed his shirt in three days. There was still a mustard stain on the lapel.

"Listen, I'm asking you to leave."

"And I'm asking you to fuck off."

With that said, the man walked away and Jack tapped the bar with his knuckles. "Let's get that drink."

The bartender looked hesitant but not wanting to knock heads, she pulled over a shot glass and filled it. Jack was about to scoop it up when he felt a hand on his shoulder. He looked ahead in the mirror and saw a beefy security guard.

"Okay, fella, time to head out."

"Sure, let me have my drink."

"No, it's time to leave."

Jack picked it up and tossed it back, he shrugged the man's hand off his shoulder and then asked the lady to fill it up again.

"I said it's time to leave."

Now on any other day, under any other conditions he would have obliged but he was in no mood for dealing with a snooty concierge or a wannabe officer.

"Give me ten minutes and I'll head out."

He placed his hand on Jack's shoulder and in one smooth motion, Jack spun and locked his arm around the security guard's back causing him to lean forward in pain. He could have kicked his feet out from underneath him but in the position he had him in, it wasn't required. He wasn't looking to disable the guy, just keep him at arm's length.

The concierge tried to intervene. "I'm calling the cops."

"No need. He's with me."

Right then, across the room came the familiar voice of his mother. She was standing at the entrance to the restaurant.

"Ma'am, I must—"

"I have a room and he's a guest. I apologize, he lost his

father today."

Jack's eyebrow shot up and he released his grip on the guard and let him slip down to the ground. The concierge's eyes darted back and forth between them, unsure of what to say or do.

Liz walked over and handed the clerk a hundred-dollar bill. "For your trouble."

He looked as if he was about to say something but instead just observed as she took a hold of Jack's arm and guided him away.

"Come on, son, let's go."

Regardless of how he felt about her, he was grateful that she stepped in when she had. At the rate he was going he was liable to end up seeing the inside of a jail cell. As they exited the internal restaurant she led him outside the hotel.

"I thought you bought a room?"

"I lied," she said.

He shook his head.

"Where we going?"

"You need a place for the evening, right?"

Several pedestrians walked by them, a cab pulled up and asked them if they needed a ride. Liz waved the cabbie away.

"I can find my own room."

"I'm sure you can but I don't live far from here and well, I think there are a few things you might want to see before you write me off."

They walked a short distance to a paid parking lot and approached a black BMW sedan. It looked brand-new. She eyed him checking it out as she got in the driver's side. The interior was leather and it was kitted out with all the typical features to be found in the high-priced 7 Series model.

They drove for about thirty minutes to the west side of L.A. to a place called Pacific Palisades. It was an affluent neighborhood close to Santa Monica State Beach. As they pulled up to the breathtaking property, he wondered what his mother did for a living. The three-story home with balconies on every level looked as if it was made for a large family or someone extremely wealthy. She pressed a button on a device attached to the sun visor and one of three garage doors opened and she eased in the vehicle.

Once inside the home, Jack took in the sight of the dark walnut wood floors, high-end marble and tile kitchen and soaring cathedral ceilings.

"Who else lives here?"

"Just me on this lower floor, Noah and his girlfriend are on the second. We are considering renting out some of the upper level. Perhaps you'd like to stay?"

He shook his head as he continued to browse. "I've never been one for settling down."

She tossed the keys on a counter and a white and gray cat came into the room. She took a second to greet it before heading into the kitchen and opening the balcony doors. Every room looked relaxing. The walls were an off-white, along with the furniture. The smell of the Pacific Ocean drifted in, along with the sound of waves and people enjoying the beach.

"Can I get you a drink?"

"Water's fine."

He walked out onto the balcony and took in the sight of it all. Outside, a clear blue sky, barely a cloud in sight, kissed a glistening ocean. Surfers rode the waves, while families sunbathed and others splashed around in the shallow waters. He walked back in and spotted a photo of Liz and Noah on a side table. She returned holding a clear glass and handed it to him.

"That was taken a year ago."

"In Florida?"

She frowned. "That's right."

"I know the location. I lived there for a while."

Thoughts of Isabel rushed back in and he placed the frame back down. In the photo Liz was drinking an orange juice. Noah looked different, as if he had packed on more weight and muscle.

"So, you married?"

"I was. It didn't last."

"If you don't mind me saying, you don't look as if you are hurting for money."

"No," she gazed around the room taking stock of her possessions, perhaps considering their value.

"Must be nice."

She smiled. "Come, let's sit in the living room."

She led him through to an equally beautiful room that had an alcove with two striped chairs, and a small rosewood table. The table was stacked with six books all to do with home décor and positive thinking.

"What do you do for a living?" Jack asked, sipping at his drink.

"Real estate."

He pursed his lips. "Um, doing well?"

"You could say so."

"And Noah?"

"Noah got involved in real estate for a while but it wasn't his thing. He dabbled for a while in owning his own surf shop but got restless when he hit his thirties. He was always talking about making a difference in the world. You know, adding depth to his life. Doing something that helped others."

"So he found religion?"

"What, because he went on a mission?" She scoffed. "Noah is far from the religious type. You don't need religion to do good to others, I'm sure you know, right, Jack?"

He wasn't sure what she was implying but he kind of figured that Dalton had been running off at the mouth again, no doubt filling her in on what he was up to from time to time.

Jack looked out the window, in the reflection he could see his mother staring at him. He hadn't considered what it must have been like for her. To finally meet the son she had left behind so many years ago.

"Tell me about you," she leaned forward a little and set her glass down then brought her hands together as if interested.

He scoffed. "What part do you want to know? The bad part, or the bad part?"

She smiled. "Can't all be bad."

"Depends who you talk to."

Liz gnawed at her lip. "Wait here a second, I want to show you something."

She left the room and Jack glanced at the magazines before looking outside. Beyond the window a neighbor was watering his flowerbed. A grandfather clock ticked quietly in the background. There was peacefulness to the place and though he didn't know her, he was glad she had found a smidgen of happiness after what she had been through.

About five minutes later Liz returned holding a shoebox in her hand. She set it on her lap and removed the top and then handed him several piles of old photos. As Jack thumbed through them he noticed that many were of her and Eddie Carmine.

"Those were taken before you were born. He was a good man, Eddie, kindhearted."

"Did he ever tell you what he did for a living?" Jack asked.

"Of course, why do you think he visited Los Angeles?"

"John told me it was because he helped his mother."

"And he did but that's not why he was out here."

Jack regarded her with curiosity. There was so much that Eddie hadn't told him and perhaps that was for the best. Who knew what would have happened to his mother if those that he'd worked for had got wind of her existence.

"I don't understand. Why did you leave us behind and not Noah?"

"Noah was born a year after I left."

"Eddie's?"

She nodded, then handed him a few more photos. This time they were of her and Kyle. That pretty much ruled out she was making this up. Jack shook his head as he stared at the image of the man he had grown to resent and detest. He barely ever mentioned his name.

"You know Eddie killed him?"

She nodded but said nothing.

"Why do you keep these?"

"To remind myself of why I left." She then pulled out a few more and the next ones weren't as pleasant to look at. They were snapshots of her arms, throat, face and legs. Bruises, cuts and burns covered them.

"He did this?"

"Kyle, yeah."

Jack's hand tightened as flashbacks of his youth came to him. The beatings and the shouting, the times he went without food and the nights he escaped to Eddie's and the final night that saw him beaten so bad he could barely stand. Jack handed back the photos. She then opened the second box. Jack was hesitant to look. He'd seen enough. However, the next batch of photos caused him to stare blankly, before looking at her. They were photos of a younger Jack and Milly in good times. Photos that Eddie had taken as they grew up. Birthdays, Christmas, Easter, and just random days when Eddie had taken time to be with them and treat them the way a father should have.

"He sent you all these?"

"Over the years. Yeah."

She swallowed hard. He could see tears welling up in her eyes and Jack handed over the photos and got up to get fresh air. Dealing with this was harder than he thought. He'd often wondered what life would have been like if his mother was alive. For the longest time, he assumed she was dead. Out on the balcony, a gentle wind whipped against his face and he held back deep-seated emotions. It wasn't like him to let them bubble up. He'd spent the better part of his life suppressing his emotion out of necessity. Emotions meant weakness in the eyes of those he ran with, and yet he was human, regardless.

From behind him he heard his mother approach.

"I'm sorry, Jack. If I could turn back time, I would... well..."

It wasn't like he could fault her. He'd made his own mistakes. Suffered brutality just like her. Walked down the same road. Chosen to turn his back on those who could have helped him and made excuses for many questionable deeds.

In his eyes, everyone was dealt a hand. Good or bad, it didn't matter. All that mattered was learning how to play it. Some were better at it, others tossed in their hand and cashed out but a few took a gamble. That was him. A man with a gambler's heart. He'd lived his whole life waiting on the next card.

Jack gripped the white railing. His mind was awash with memories of the past and questions about the future. Twenty-four hours ago, he assumed there was no one left in his life. Now he faced a crossroad. A dilemma.

"Tell me more about this prison," Jack said.

Five - Capital Murder

Forty-eight hours later, a Boeing 737 made an approach to land at Toncontín Airport in Honduras. It was considered one of the world's most dangerous landings thanks in part to the mountainous region and short runway. Jack gripped the armrest expecting the worst.

He glanced out the small oval window at the city of Tegucigalpa as the plane banked sharply. The engines roared, threatening to cut out as they made the tricky descent. A maze of shanties and huts surrounded by lush tropical jungle and jagged mountains rose.

Over the period of two days he'd gone back and forth on whether to help or not. It wasn't a case of not being willing. This wasn't like just going into a city or country and trying to find someone, or banging on doors and breaking bones to get answers. There were only three ways someone got out of a third world prison before their allotted time: bribery, escape or high-priced lawyers who knew a few loopholes in the justice system. Liz had already exhausted one of those methods. The lawyer she hired was so restrained by red tape that the chances of getting Noah out were slim to none. He'd handed back what she'd paid him and written off Noah. When asked if the prison officials could be bribed, he made it clear in no uncertain terms that while it had worked for some in the past it rarely worked now because no matter what was offered, they would always ask for more. It was true. In their eyes, every American was wealthy. It was the reason so many Americans ended up trapped inside a foreign prison system. It was a nightmare.

Still, the alternative of trying to break him out was a last resort and one he wasn't even considering. At least, not until he had exhausted other options. Jack figured he would offer fifty thousand dollars, if they wanted more he could go up to one hundred, beyond that he'd have to consider other means.

As the tires touched down and the brakes screeched,

making the steel coffin shudder, he jerked around in his seat hoping they didn't overshoot the landing. It had happened before. There had been several incidents, all of which came down to human error.

"Good morning, this is your captain speaking. I would like to thank you for flying with us. The latest Honduras weather is cloudy skies, temperature twenty-nine degrees – that's 84 Fahrenheit. We expect to have you on your way in approximately ten minutes. Please remain in your seats as we make the final preparations. Again, on behalf of all of us we would like to thank you for flying with us today and we hope the next time your travel plans call for a trip to Honduras you will choose American Airlines. Have a very pleasant stay in the Tegucigalpa area and a safe journey home."

* * *

After collecting his one duffel bag, and making it through security, he stepped out into the morning sunshine and glanced at the collection of white taxis vying for attention. Most of the drivers were standing outside their vehicle smoking and trying to coax people to use their service. Jack made eye contact with one and he was over faster than a jackrabbit.

He already had his hands on his bag. "Sir, let me take your bag. Where do you want to go?"

Jack released it and watched as he tossed it into the trunk and then slid around to the driver's side. He looked around for a second before slipping in.

"Danlí."

He twisted around in his seat. "That's over two hours away."

"And?"

"You have money?"

Jack wasn't going to flash it. He'd heard horror stories of travelers flashing money only to end up facedown in some dingy back alley in God knows where with a bullet in the skull. Instead, he nodded. The man didn't look convinced so Jack reached in and thumbed off a few hundred-dollar bills and handed them over.

"Enough?"

His eyes lit up and he snatched them out of his hands like a greedy child. "All right, let's go." The engine purred to life, he donned a pair of cheap sunglasses and cranked the tunes. They zipped out into a stream of traffic and began making the long journey east.

"I'm Mario Francisco, and you are?"

"Tired," Jack replied.

"Ah, long flight. What part of America are you from?"

Jack closed his eyes and tried his best to tune out the drone. The guy couldn't take a hint as he just went to the next question even if the previous one was unanswered.

"I have a cousin in Florida. Are you from Florida?"

"Close."

"And what brings you to Honduras?"

"A brother."

"Ah, what's he do? Business? Missions?"

"Prison."

Jack glanced up to see him staring at him in the rearview mirror.

"You want to keep your eyes on the road," Jack said

noticing that he was about to plow into the back of a construction truck. He turned just in time and veered left without even looking to see who was in the next lane. That was how they drove. There was no road etiquette. No waiting around or giving someone else a turn. It was every man for himself. Drivers pulled their vehicles out into oncoming traffic, forcing others to slow or honk their horns.

"Don't worry, we'll make it there alive. The most common accidents occur because people go over the edge of cliffs on some of the narrow roads."

"Is that so," Jack muttered trying to get comfy but his voice was beginning to grate on his nerves.

"Yep. No barriers. Our government is poor and can barely afford to repair the roads."

That was clearly evident by the large potholes all over the road. He bounced several times in his seat. It was like the surface of the moon. Most of the secondary roads were unpaved, nothing more than dirt trails and rock.

"In the rainy season, my job is a nightmare. The

government closes a lot of the roads because there are so many rock slides, flash flooding and so on."

"You heard of Danlí Prison?" Jack asked. If the guy was going to rattle on, he was going to steer the conversation towards something that was useful.

"Who hasn't? Terrible place, worst one in Honduras," he said before glancing up at his mirror. "Is that where your brother is?"

Jack gave a short nod.

He shook his head while tapping against the steering wheel. "That's not good. No sir. That's not. Inmates die in there all the time."

"From the guards?"

He snorted. "No sir. The inmates run the place."

"What?"

"Oh yeah, after a riot a few years back the guards reached a truce with the inmates. They are the ones that now run the interior. Many of them are armed."

"Armed inmates? C'mon, you're bullshitting me."

"No, sir. My sister's cousin is in there. He says some of

73

them carry batons."

"How many inmates?"

"Last I heard, seven hundred."

"That's not many."

He laughed. "For a place that is only meant to house two hundred and forty, that's too many. The compound is as cramped as fuck."

"How many guards?"

"Why, you thinking of breaking him out?" He snorted and laughed a little before replying. "Twelve."

Jack's eyebrows shot up. "Twelve guards to watch over them?"

"No, they employ others but there is only twelve on a shift. They are armed with machine guns but they leave the inmates to handle internal problems because of overcrowding. So there is no need for any more."

Twelve on shift? He couldn't wrap his head around that.

It seemed unreal but the system in Honduras was far different than in the States. Arming the inmates with batons would have never been allowed in the U.S. but in a country that had over four hundred deaths a month, spent only a dollar a day to feed each prisoner, and survived on bribes, it was to be expected. It was a defunct government that hadn't shaken its reputation of being the murder capital of the world.

Six - Gold Teeth

Traveling through the hot spot of danger didn't make him feel comfortable. He'd had to travel without a gun and after hearing even more horror stories from Mario, he was wondering if he'd made the right decision. Jack leaned his head against the window and bumped around in the back as Mario shared his life story. He thought back to what Liz had said the day before he left to remind himself of why he was doing it.

"He'll die in there, Jack."

Jack put his beer down on the small table between them. They were sitting outside on the balcony. It was evening. All along the beach, the glow of lights from homes made it feel like Christmas.

"He stands as much chance as anyone else."

"You don't know what it's like."

He chuckled at that. "I spent the better part of four years in prison, most of which were spent in solitary confinement. I think I know."

"This isn't any ordinary U.S. prison where people have rights."

"Rights? Where the hell were my rights? One hour a day in the courtyard wasn't right."

"But you made it through. Noah isn't made for this. Besides... he says there are fights being held there for money. People are dying every week."

"Fighting comes with the territory."

"Perhaps, but internal fighting that is condoned by the warden doesn't."

Jack shot her a sideways glance. She nodded. "I spoke with Noah a week ago. He's scared, Jack."

"So get your lawyer to work his magic."

"What do you think I'm doing? I'm already paying through the nose to ensure that no harm comes to him while he tries to work through all the legal bullshit." She shook her head and wiped away a tear that trickled down the right side of her face.

"Hell, I don't know if he's even doing anything. I spoke

with him yesterday and it's always the same. It's slow. It takes time. He has other clients that are in dire situations just like Noah. Even if you could just go down there and check in on him, perhaps you can see what is being done. I need to know there is light at the end of the tunnel, cause right now I don't see it."

She got up and took her empty beer bottle back into the kitchen and returned with a yellow package. She set it down beside his beer.

"What's that?" Jack asked.

"John told me about what you did for a living. There is fifty thousand in there."

He frowned. "I don't want your money."

"Then use it to bribe them. Maybe they'll turn a blind eye for the right price."

"Fifty thousand will not cut it. You go flashing that around and they will want more."

"Then how much?"

Jack slid the package back across the table to her. He shook his head as he looked out at the reflection of the moon *on the water. The sloshing of waves against the shore was mesmerizing, almost beckoning him.*

"I'll go see what I can do, but I can't guarantee anything."

"I understand."

Mario slammed on the brakes and cursed some driver that had darted out in front of him. The sudden jolt brought him back into the present moment.

"Get the hell out of the way!" He smashed the horn multiple times, then veered around the truck that had tried to squeeze in between the taxi and the vehicle ahead.

"You have the address for the place in Danlí?"

Jack fished around in his jacket for the scrap of paper that Liz had jotted down the lawyer's address on. It took another twenty minutes before they reached the destination. When they arrived, Jack expected to find a run-down, dilapidated building that was being used by multiple lawyers to cover the cost of rent. Instead, he was dropped off at a large factory with a sign that read Honduran-Cuban Tobacco Company.

"Are you sure this is the right place?"

Mario picked the paper back up again and gazed out his windshield towards a green sign.

"This is it."

"Odd. You think you could stick around?"

"Payment first."

Jack reached in and thumbed off a few more bills. "I'll park over there and catch a few winks. If I'm not in the vehicle, just check the bar across the street."

Jack exited the vehicle and headed inside the factory. He was greeted by the sight of seventy or more workers hand rolling cigars. There were close to fifty tables full of piles of dried tobacco leaf. A few of the women looked over while continuing to work. A man seated behind a desk sign that read Honduras Cigars Hand Made caught his gaze before continuing to examine large cigars that he was placing in a box. He was wearing a brown leather cowboy hat, blue denim shirt and white pants. He had a cigar sticking out from beneath his thick black mustache.

"I'm looking for someone by the name of José Breve.

Would you know where I can find him?"

The man lowered his glasses and looked at him.

"That depends, who's asking?"

"I'm here on behalf of Liz Matthews."

His eyes lit up and he swallowed. He rose to his feet. "I'm José."

Jack frowned and José registered it.

"Oh this?" he thumbed over his shoulder. "I like to be involved in the work of my company. Yep, the reason so many good companies get a bad reputation is they grow too fast and the owners distance themselves from the business. I have had this running for over six years and it will continue for another six as long as I take care of the end product."

He motioned to the table. "Just doing a little bit of quality control."

"But you're a lawyer?"

"That I am."

José could tell he was struggling to understand why he was working for a cigar company.

"There is a saying in Honduras. Everyone needs a lawyer but everyone can't afford one." He then laughed and extended his hand. "And you are?"

"Jack Winchester. Liz's son."

It felt weird saying it and yet normal.

"Ah, I should have guessed. You look like Noah."

"That's what Liz says. I don't see the resemblance."

"I can tell."

José looked past him and then gazed down at his backpack. "Where are you staying?"

"I haven't selected a hotel."

"I can recommend a few good ones. Safe." He turned and walked towards a section of the building that contained offices. Jack stood where he was. "You coming?" José asked.

Jack readjusted his bag and followed him. He closed the office door behind him and pulled the blinds down. "Like I told Liz, these matters are very delicate. You can't force things here. At least not without a large amount of money." He grinned and Jack noticed that several of his teeth were gold.

"So you operate your lawyer business from here?"

"No, I have an office three blocks from here but I'm rarely there. Few people are beating down my door, most phone from prison."

Jack gestured to a stack of cigar boxes. "You sell a lot of these cigars?"

"Most orders come from the U.S., though I have a few contacts in the San Pedro Sula and Guatemala region. But enough about what I do. Liz never mentioned she would send anyone. Is there a problem?"

"Not that I know of. No, she wanted to try a different approach. She thought because you have already established a connection with the prison, that you could get me in to speak with the warden."

José smiled and leaned back in his seat. "Ah, smart lady. And may I ask how much she sent?"

"We can discuss numbers when you have made an appointment."

He huffed. "I would need to know in advance. The

warden is a busy man and he doesn't open his door for just anyone. He needs a good reason."

"How's fifty thousand dollars sound?"

Seven - Trouble Brewing

José's ears perked up at the mention of cold hard cash. He leaned forward in his chair and regarded Jack with skepticism. He picked at a gold tooth with a thin wooden pick, then took a large toke on his cigar. Jack kind of figured he would want to see it and he didn't plan on flashing it around.

Without saying another word José reached for the phone on his desk and placed a call. His voice was hushed as he spoke. Jack gazed around at the various stone sculptures he had. On the wall were several awards for cigars he had manufactured, and one related to his work as a lawyer. One that caught his attention was of a school. There were several teachers in the photo along with about fifty children.

"I built that school," José said. Jack turned to find him staring and holding a hand over the receiver. "Cost twenty grand for the building, furniture, equipment, books and the fence around it."

"Twenty thousand goes a long way."

"So does fifty."

After a couple of minutes he hung up. "I've arranged an appointment for this afternoon."

"That soon?"

"Money speaks around these parts." He stood up and came over. "In the meantime, can I give you a ride to a hotel? I recommend the Hotel Casa Encantada."

"I have a ride outside but thank you."

José glanced out the window.

"The taxi?"

Jack nodded before glancing at his watch. It was a little after eleven in the morning.

"Meet me here at two," José said. "I'll take you to see Lázaro."

Jack thanked him for his time and exited. He cast a glance over his shoulder and saw José was back on the phone.

Mario wasn't to be found in his vehicle, so Jack jogged

across the street to a sports bar. He adjusted the bag on his shoulder as he stepped inside. It wasn't much to look at inside, a few tables, bar stools and a simple bar with a fridge full of foreign beer. Mario was sitting at the far end talking to a young girl. Some trashy pop song was playing on low in the background. The bartender tossed him a glance as he passed by.

He tapped him on the arm. "Mario, time to go."

"Ah, I was just telling Kelyn here about your visit to Honduras. She says we could join her and some of her friends if you're interested."

"Not interested. Let's go."

He tugged on his shirt and Mario said his farewell.

"You know, Jack, women like that are hard to come across in the city. For a few dollars, you and I could have one hell of a night."

"No time. I have business to attend to."

Mario still had a beer in his hand.

"You allowed to drink and drive?"

He laughed. "Half the people on the road are drunk."

Well that explained the crazy driving.

They had just made their way back to the taxi and Jack was waiting for him to unlock the doors when five guys made their way across the street. Two were still drinking and they didn't appear to be looking to hail a cab.

A few words were muttered in Spanish. Sensing trouble, Mario put his hands up and fired back a few words.

The next thing Jack knew, Mario was struck across the head with a bottle and then another guy tried to grab Jack's backpack. Jack held it tight and backhanded the guy. After which all hell broke loose. A bottle was smashed on the hood of the taxi and a guy came at Jack holding the shattered neck. He thrust forward and Jack sidestepped to the right, kicking him in the stomach. Meanwhile Mario was getting the shit kicked out of him by two guys.

The jagged bottle came at him again and this time, Jack swung his bag and then fired a right hook that knocked his attacker clean off his feet. One thing about these Honduran people, they weren't exactly built for battle. It was like hitting a feather. He followed through with a sharp kick to the nuts. He let out a groan and doubled over. Jack grabbed the next guy by the back of the neck and unloaded two jabs to the stomach only to have someone kick him from behind. His bag dropped to the floor. As he scrambled to get up, one man took a running kick. Jack grabbed the guy's leg, twisted and yanked it towards him, causing the guy to lose his balance. Out the corner of his eye, he saw the first guy dart in, scoop up his bag and sprint away. Wasting no time, he raced after him around a section of stores, across a street and down through the narrow streets. The guy gave a fearful glance over his shoulder. He vaulted over a fence, and tossed several trashcans at Jack but he kept moving forward. As they raced past a construction site, Jack eyed a pile of loose bricks, he scooped one up as he shot by and took aim while running after him. A few seconds later, the guy hit the ground with a gnarly gash to the back of his head. Out of breath and ready to lay down a serious beating, Jack grabbed up his bag and opted instead to just give the guy a quick kick in the gut.

"Asshole," Jack muttered while curious onlookers watched on.

By the time he jogged back to where the taxi had been, it was gone and Mario was lying motionless with a pool of blood around his abdomen. A crowd had formed, and several people were shouting in Spanish. Jack squeezed his way through the crowd to take in the sight of the cheerful guy who was alive and well only moments earlier. A police siren could be heard wailing in the distance. Locals scattered as if expecting to be carted away for just being at the scene of a crime.

Jack remained there looking down.

"Jack!" a male voice called out to him. He turned to find José beckoning him towards his factory while casting a nervous glance up and down the street. Once he made it over, José pulled him in and locked up the front door. A police vehicle screeched to halt not far from the body and several officers carrying semi-automatic weapons jumped out, fanning in multiple directions.

The fear among the people was tangible.

Jack peered out through a slot in the door. An ambulance roared into view, sirens blared and lights flashed. A mishmash of blue and red. It all happened so fast.

"You don't want to go out there for a while."

"This happen a lot?"

He chuckled. "More than you know."

Eight - The Warden

Jack skipped booking into the hotel. José promised to take him there later once they'd been to see the warden. Instead, they slipped out back and traveled to his home twenty minutes away. He spent the following hour on a guided tour of the place. Glass was embedded into the top of the walls and three vicious Rottweilers roamed the inner courtyard. Over lunch he shared some of the cases he'd had, those that had failed and others that were a success. One thing he made clear was that the justice system worked very differently from the one back in the States. Rights were a joke down there. Had Jack been caught out in the open when Mario died, he would have ended up being brought before the court and sentenced within forty-eight hours. Judgment was swift and punishment far worse.

"Have you bought out an inmate?"

He nodded, puffing on his cigar and patting the head

of a snarling dog that had been eyeing Jack for the past quarter of an hour. It looked as if it was just waiting for the attack command.

"Are those necessary?"

"Without a doubt. Home invasions are very common down here. Police don't go out to every call. Hell, sometimes the police are involved. Dozens of officers have helped gangs by deleting gang members' records and providing them with fake driving licenses for big money. Just a few months back, thirteen out of sixty-seven police officers were on the payroll of a powerful gang that operated here in Honduras. They took ages to push that one through the court system. Judges get paid off all the time. And because you never know which cops are involved in extortion, murder, bank robberies, auto theft, kidnapping and drug trafficking, you can't stick around at a crime scene. That's why people are afraid when they hear them coming. The people here have huge trust issues. But I'm sure you get that back in the USA."

Jack chewed away on some melon that was stacked on

his plate. "It happens. It's not as common but dirty cops exist."

"You are taking a big risk coming down here, and an even greater one carrying around the money in that sack of yours."

Jack stared back at him.

"I saw you run after him. No one runs after anyone down here unless there is value or they want to die."

"Perhaps I want to die."

"That can be arranged," he said with a smile. "Stick around here long enough and your wish may be granted." He paused for a second to take a hard pull on a long, fat cigar. The end burned hot. A smile flickered on his face as he waved away the gray smoke. "You know, your brother is not the first American that has been pulled in for drug trafficking. It happens a lot."

"Makes little sense. Why would anyone place drugs in his bag? They must have known he would get searched at the airport. It's a dumb way to try and get drugs into the USA."

"Who's to say they were trying to get it into the USA? Perhaps they needed to get it out of the area. Maybe they would take it back when he reached the airport. There are many reasons they might have done it."

While he was speaking, another man came into the room and whispered into his ear. "Superb, Carlos, get the car ready," José said, then turned back to Jack. "You ready to meet Lázaro?"

* * *

For whatever reason Lázaro Torres chose not to meet at the prison. Whether he thought the place was under surveillance or he didn't spend that much time there was anyone's guess. The journey was a short ride out to a home on the south side of Danlí. It was in an upscale neighborhood similar to José's, yet even more extravagant. For someone that worked for the government, his two-story villa seemed a bit extravagent.

The winding road that led up to the property gave them a breathtaking view of the valley. Only the wealthy could own such homes in the area. That was the thing about Honduras, or any third world country. A person could drive through the slums but then within twenty minutes be basking in the glory of wealth.

Once they parked, José was clear about letting him do all the talking.

As they ascended the steps up to the stone terrace, Jack caught sight of a silver-haired man with a thick beard. He sat at a table reading a newspaper, with a cup of coffee in front of him. He wore a white shirt, and black pants. He noticed them but continued to read even as they approached. They must have stood there for a few minutes until he folded his paper.

José greeted him in Spanish but he replied in English. It wasn't perfect but it was clear enough to carry on a conversation.

"Lázaro, this is Jack Winchester."

"Take a seat. Can I get you some coffee, juice, perhaps?"

"Coffee would be good."

Lázaro motioned to a butler and he disappeared inside.

"How is business, José?"

"Can't complain."

"I heard there was an incident outside your factory."

His eyes drifted over to Jack who stared at him before turning away.

"Nothing that the police weren't able to handle."

"And so you wanted to see me about an inmate?"

José spoke again in Spanish. Jack knew enough Spanish to understand what he was saying. There was mention of the money. His brother's name was dropped and that they were looking to reach an agreement.

"José, English. I'm sure your friend here would like to understand."

"I understand well enough, thank you," Jack replied, to which Lázaro smirked.

"Fifty thousand for the release of your brother?"

Jack nodded.

"That's a lot of money. Under any other circumstances, I would be more than obliged to come to an agreement. It's rare that we get any Americans in Danlí

Prison and those that we do aren't able to offer such a lucrative amount. Though, I have to ask myself, is it worth it? I mean with the judicial system breathing down on our necks, I need time to weigh up the pros and cons."

"Is it not enough?" Jack asked.

"Why, are you offering more?"

"Look, let's not jerk each other off. What is it going to take to get him out?"

Lázaro ran a hand over his mouth and smiled.

"Fifty thousand is a nice round figure, except he is worth more inside."

Jack screwed up his face. "How so?"

"You're not familiar with the way things work down here, are you?"

"Not exactly."

Lázaro shrugged. "As much as I like you, Mr. Winchester, I'm afraid I cannot help you."

"Seventy-five thousand."

"Mr. Winchester."

"A hundred and that's it."

He snorted and took a sip of his coffee. "That's a lot of money to be carrying around even for a man like yourself."

He had to wonder what he meant by that. He didn't know him unless he'd had him under surveillance from the moment he stepped off the plane. It wouldn't have been the first time he'd seen a criminal element keep tabs on foreigners arriving. Word traveled faster, even faster if those working for the airport were connected to gangs or the warden. Though more than likely, José had seen him fight and he was referring to his ability to protect his property.

Jack was done with vague figures. Money spoke volumes when seen. He pulled his bag around and was about to unzip it when two men stepped forward with their Glocks raised.

He raised a hand. "Just getting the money out."

"You must excuse my men. They get a little nervous around strangers."

Jack unzipped the bag and pulled out one hundred

thousand all in hundred-dollar bills and wrapped in several bags. He placed them in front of him and Lázaro glanced at them before picking one up, peeling off the wrapping and thumbing his way through it.

"I still need time to think about this. Our prison has been under review as of late and if I move ahead, it must be dealt with in a manner that doesn't bring into question the initial decision of the Danlí courthouse. You understand?"

Jack nodded and went to take the money back. Lázaro placed his hand on top of it.

"It stays here."

Jack screwed up his face.

"Don't worry. You have my word. If I decide to not go ahead, you will receive the money back."

"No offense but after what happened today, I have trust issues."

He laughed. "I like him, José." Lázaro bit down on his lower lip. "Okay, but I will keep hold of fifty thousand, a deposit so I know you are serious and not wasting my time."

Jack looked at José and raised an eyebrow.

"Do we have a deal, Mr. Winchester?"

Jack released his hand from the money and gave a curt nod.

Nine - Night Raid

Later as Jack checked in at the Hotel Casa Encantada for the evening, the afternoon's meeting with Lázaro preoccupied his mind. He wasn't comfortable leaving half the money with him but at this stage he had few options. José had treated him to a meal at some fancy steakhouse in Danlí before dropping him off at the hotel. On the surface, everything appeared to be fine. José tried to ease his concerns about the warden backing out, or stealing his money. He assured him that wasn't how it worked. The warden had to be careful.

Hotel Casa Encantada was just as gorgeous as described. Though it wasn't up to the standard of American hotels, it looked better than some of the bug-infested motels he'd seen so far.

It was Mexican in appearance and almost reminded him of the structures seen in old Western movies. A two-story building with a wraparound balcony. Everything was made from a deep red wood. The rooms were basic but comfortable and clean. It offered all he needed. A double bed, tiled floors, a stunning bathroom and a TV. If he hadn't heard from Lázaro within twenty-four hours he would collect the money and look at alternative options for getting Noah out. How? He had no idea. A lot was riding on the fact that the system was defunct and they were open to bribery. What José had shared about the police being dirty was a good sign. It meant that the chance of being able to get Noah out was high.

Jack called down to the front desk and asked for room service to bring up a bottle of beer as they had no mini fridge in the room. He took a quick shower, keeping an eye out for roaches. Though it looked clean enough, he wasn't convinced that it was bug-free. He'd seen one crawl across the floor in the reception area.

Once he cleaned up he placed a phone call to Liz to update her on the situation. She'd persuaded him to take the fifty thousand and use it, and he had contributed some of his own. He kind of figured that they would want top dollar for an American.

"No, it's okay, I have made the arrangements."

"Jack, I can't thank you enough."

"Well don't break out the bubbly yet. I'm still waiting to hear from him."

"You don't think he will pull out, do you?"

"Anything is possible down here."

Jack didn't want to tell her about how his taxi driver's life had been snuffed out. She had enough on her plate as it was.

"When this is over, will you stick around?"

"I don't know about that," Jack replied.

"Just a few weeks. I want to get to know you more, and I'm sure Noah will."

"I'll think about it."

There was a knock at the door. "Just hold the line a second."

"Come in."

There was no response.

Jack set the phone on the bed and crossed the room.

He opened the door expecting one concierge to be holding a bottle of beer. Instead, he was greeted by two M4 barrels shoved in his face. The next thing he knew he was being thrust back inside and tossed down to the ground.

"Policía."

"What is going on?"

They continued to speak in Spanish.

"I don't understand."

He understood a few of the words they were spitting out but as several of them were speaking at once he couldn't make head or tails of it. He caught something about the taxi driver, and then they had him on his front and were handcuffing him. Meanwhile several officers ransacked the room. One of them held up his bag and said he had it.

"You are under arrest for the murder of Mario Francisco."

They read him his rights but he knew he had none. They hauled him up off the ground and shoved him outside. Curious guests and staff looked on as they strong-armed him down to the ground and then out to a waiting cruiser. Jack was tossed into the back and the door slammed behind him. It all happened in a matter of minutes. They were fast, and weren't messing around. Sirens wailed, and the lights cut into the night as they peeled away. He couldn't believe this was happening. He considered trying to get out of the cuffs but it wouldn't have helped. He was in a foreign country, they had his money and passport. No, he would ride this out and see if he could get in contact with José or Lázaro, perhaps they could get him out of this mess.

The police department was a straight shot down N-53, about ten minutes away. They stopped outside a bright yellow building with the words Policía Nacional Danlí engraved above the doorway. He was forced out of the cruiser and shoved through a door and brought into the station. All the cops were paramilitary. Those that had brought him in had balaclavas on to hide the lower half of their faces, bulletproof vests and were packing submachine guns. Again he heard several different officers barking orders in Spanish. Once they stripped him of his shoes and socks, they escorted him into a cell and locked it. The cell wasn't empty. He was sharing it with five locals. Jack banged on the bars. "I get a phone call. Hey! Hey!"

A door slammed behind him and there was quiet, only the sound of someone snoring on a bench while the others looked on. A large guy rose from his seat and eyed Jack with a menacing look. He wore a tank top and his arms were twice the size of Jack's legs. The others looked like tweakers, with sunken eyes and acting all paranoid.

He sighed.

It would be a long night.

Ten - Witness

When sunshine flooded the cramped cell the next morning, Jack was still awake. It wasn't because he feared the other prisoners; it was that he couldn't get his mind to shut off. He figured that when they brought him out and gave him his phone call, he would have it all cleared up and be on his way by noon. Or was that wishful thinking?

As he squatted on a cold hard floor, the thump of boots coming his way was a welcome sound. A guard rattled his baton against the bars and unlocked the dungeon-style enclosure. He pointed at Jack and told him to step out. He glanced at the others and they gave a nod. Tired, hungry and smelling like shit, all he wanted to do was take a shower and get eight hours' sleep. But that wasn't happening.

Guided out into a busy office, he was relieved to see José. He was dressed in a tan suit and tie and looking a hell of a lot more professional than he had the first time he met him. He was talking to one officer and laughing as they strolled up.

"Ah Jack," he said before extending his hand. "I was telling them that this has been a big misunderstanding."

"About time."

"Unfortunately, they aren't buying it and have said they have multiple witnesses that place you at the scene of the incident, stabbing the taxi driver."

"What?"

He put out a hand to calm him down. "I know. I know. I told them it was absurd but they still want to bring you before a lineup of witnesses."

"Just tell them I was with you."

"That's the thing. I only saw you after he was dead."

"But you know I didn't kill him."

"I know. Well I mean, I believe you but the odds are stacked against you right now as several witnesses said that they saw you stab him."

"I'm being set up," Jack said running a hand over his unshaven face. It was one thing to be told that he murdered someone, another to be thrown to the wolves. What were the chances that the witnesses saw any other American-looking male in the area at the time?

"Look, just get in the lineup and worst-case scenario, we'll tackle it in court."

"Right. As that worked well for my brother."

He threw up a hand. "The justice system is what it is. You have money, right?"

Jack snorted. "You mean the other fifty thousand? No! They took it with them. It's probably been put towards beer."

An officer came over and muttered something in José's ear and he nodded. "He wants you to go with him. It shouldn't take too long. Don't worry, Jack, I'll get this all smoothed out."

Jack stared back at him as he was grabbed by the arm and led off down the corridor towards a room. He was fucked. No matter how this played out, Lázaro had fifty thousand and a corrupt police department had the other fifty. Even if he got out of this, he would still be down fifty grand. There was no chance in hell he would see that money again.

Brought into a room, he smirked as he looked at the lineup they had brought in. It was between him, a loudmouth Irishman and a Cuban midget who wasn't even Caucasian. They were instructed to face a one-way mirror. Who was the witness? This wasn't fair treatment. Where was the evidence? Without hard proof, they couldn't do shit, could they?

They stood there for several minutes. The Irishman was belligerent and kept flipping them the bird. They couldn't have been in there for over five minutes before they were escorted out of the room. The Irishman and the midget were let go, while Jack was hauled to one side. José was already waiting to hear the outcome. It felt like everything was moving too fast. An officer came out of an adjourning room and gave a nod to José. He squeezed his eyes closed and made an expression that made it damn obvious what the verdict was.

"José?"

"The witnesses pointed you out from among the others."

"Well no shit. The other two weren't even in the vicinity. This is bullshit."

José scrubbed the corner of his eye, then pulled out a white cloth and wiped sweat from his brow.

"Look, I can help you here but my hands are tied until I know more details."

"Well what am I meant to do in the meantime?"

"Sit tight and I'll try and see what I can do."

Jack's shoulders slumped. Something didn't feel right about this.

"Don't I get a phone call or something?"

"I can arrange that, who are you going to call?"

"Lázaro."

José shook his head. "He won't get involved. It's a conflict of interest."

"Oh, but he would take a hundred thousand to release my brother? And about that, I don't have the other half, so unless he's willing to accept what he has now, the deal is off."

"Just calm down."

Jack got real close to him and an officer pulled him back. He stared José down. Together they looked like David and Goliath in size.

"Calm down? You're not the one in cuffs looking at being thrown in prison for something he didn't commit."

"It's procedure, Jack. It's what they do."

"Convicting innocent people or stealing their money? You better not be behind this."

José backed up a little. His demeanor changed real fast. "Excuse me? Are you accusing me of having some involvement in this?"

Jack shook his head, he didn't know what to think but it seemed a little convenient that the cops knew where to find him.

"Just make sure I don't go to prison."

"They won't send you to prison. There will be a trial first."

Jack scoffed. "Right, a trial. And by that you mean a

fair trial?"

"It's always fair, it might not be accurate but it's always fair."

"Bullshit. How about you get me that phone call?"

José looked uncomfortable. He pulled at his shirt collar and said he would go do that. He turned and walked away while an officer escorted Jack back to the jail cell. As he heard the key lock, a flashback of his time in Rikers tormented him.

Jack retreated to the back of the cell and eyed the new influx of men who had been squeezed into the cell only big enough for two guys. They were huddled around with their backs turned. One of the Honduran men looked over at him, his eye bruised and lip cut. He squinted for a few seconds and then got this look on his face that said he knew Jack. He was familiar. *Where have I seen you?*

Before it sunk in, the guy rose from his seat and cracked his head from side to side. Jack could see where this was heading before he even took the first shot. Jack was down at waist level when the guy lunged for him.

Jack slammed his fist into his nutsack then followed up with an uppercut. As he rose to his feet he was then attacked from the left by another guy wearing a cowboy hat. That's when he realized whom he was sharing the cell with. It was some of the same men who had attacked them outside the bar.

He felt the stab of a punch connect with his jaw. Jack slammed the guy up against the bars and kneed him repeatedly before elbowing the side of his face. No sooner had he finished than he was hauled backward and brought down to the ground. Multiple legs kicked him from every angle. Each time he tried to stand, a fist or a punch met him. Not one to cower back from a fight, he reared back both legs and plowed his feet hard into the knees of two men. They cried out in agony. Jack turned and bit another guy's leg and dragged him down to the floor like a savage animal.

The assault only lasted a few minutes before two officers unlocked the door and stormed in with batons. They lashed out and beat them on the backs, across the face and legs — it was brutal and fast but the only way to subdue an out-of-control group of prisoners.

All the while Jack had one of them on the ground by the throat and was shouting at him.

"¿Quién te contrató?"

Jack was asking who hired them. If they had been brought in after him, someone was covering their ass. He had to wonder who had paid them to attack outside the bar. Before he could get an answer, he was dragged out and the beating continued. All the while he was trying to tell the guards they were the men who killed the taxi driver.

But the police weren't listening.

Eleven - DANLÍ PRISON

Hours passed before José returned with two officers. He took one look at the bruises on Jack's face and shook his head.

"Don't worry, they look worse than me," Jack said trying to make light of the situation but nothing about what was occurring was light. Uncertainty hung over his head and based on how he'd been treated so far, the future didn't look promising.

"They will take you before Danlí Courthouse, you'll see a judge and they will decide your fate."

"Already?"

"Things move fast here."

Jack shook his head and balled his fists. "You'll be there, right?"

"Of course, but I can't guarantee anything."

As he was escorted out of the police department and loaded onto the back of a truck in handcuffs, Jack continued to ask José questions. "Surely some of the businesses in the area have cameras?"

"In America maybe. People are poor here."

"It occurred just a few buildings down from you, are you saying you have no surveillance?"

"I use guards. What's the use of cameras? They can't stop an intruder."

Jack shook his head as two officers hopped up beside him and they banged the side of the truck.

"I will see you over there."

The small white pickup truck pulled away leaving José in a cloud of exhaust fumes. It was a short distance to the courthouse. It wasn't much to look at, nothing but a cream one-story building that had an information booth in the lobby and rotating doors which led into a corridor with three rooms that were used for court appearances. José said all three were in use. The prisons in Honduras were overcrowded and there never seemed to be enough cells; that's why they would squeeze twenty or more people in one jail cell. Some would sleep on beds, others on the hard concrete floor.

As Jack was led in, the room was divided. Either side of him were seats for families and the public to listen in on a hearing. All were empty. He was made to sit in the dock until the judge came in. What occurred next seemed almost surreal. The judge stared down at the paperwork, muttered a few words in Spanish and glanced at Jack. José stood up and replied and there appeared to be a bit of back and forth regarding the circumstances, evidence and witness testimonies. Jack was sure they wouldn't have enough to convict him. When the gavel resounded and the judge left, Jack was hauled to his feet and escorted out. The entire procedure couldn't have lasted over ten minutes.

"So?" Jack asked.

"I'm sorry. You'll be escorted to Danlí Prison where you will serve out your sentence for murder."

"What?"

"Nothing I can do, at least for now. This is not over, Jack. I promise I will do whatever I can to help."

"Just like that?"

"I'm sorry."

Jack wanted to lash out at someone but cuffed and being strong-armed away, he couldn't do anything.

"And the money?"

"I will look into it."

An officer opened a door and held it wide as Jack passed through it.

"How long?"

"Nineteen years. You could be out in fifteen with good behavior. We'll try to appeal but it's not looking good."

Nineteen years? Some murderers in the USA got less than a quarter of that.

Jack was speechless. The world around him was caving in. Four years was hard enough and that was in a prison that would have been like the Ritz compared to the slum he was about to enter. José continued to talk but most of what he said just went in one ear and out the other. His mind was churning over at the thought of prison life. It still hadn't sunk in. Denial forced its way to the front of his mind, even as they loaded him into the back of the truck and José went his separate way.

Jack took in the sights of Honduras, a place that would forever be burned inside his memory. He hadn't even had the chance to tour it. Palm trees and colorful buildings were dotted all over the place. Farmers sold fruit and veggies out the back of their trucks. A thriving, lush forest swallowed up the small town stricken by poverty as they made their way to what would become his hell. The only comfort to be found was that he would finally get to meet his brother. The irony wasn't wasted.

From the moment they rolled up to the dilapidated prison grounds he could see this wouldn't be pleasant. There was no surveillance or electronic security; it functioned like a prison from the dark ages. Fences, crumbling walls and keys that locked barred doors.

The truck slowed and idled as a guard opened the flimsy chain-link fence that would give them access to the outer grounds; an area that the guards patrolled. Just across from the prison were regular stores. Old men with weathered faces sat outside observing what must have been an everyday event. How many criminals were hauled in on a daily basis? How many got out alive? A few chickens clucked beneath decaying vehicles while prison guards dressed in gray and white camo gear walked back and forth with sub-machine guns. From what Jack observed as they rolled into the grounds, sixteen-foot walls enclosed the compound itself with barbwire along the top. At two of the corners close to the front entrance were soaring guard towers. Beyond that was a vast mountain smothered by a tropical jungle.

Led in through the main entrance, Jack was met by an officer with a pad of paper. He asked for his name.

"Jack Winchester."

"Is this the first time you have been jailed?"

"Nope," he replied, his eyes fixed on the ground. After that he was led along a short corridor.

The guard motioned for him to enter a doorway. "Go through there into the showers."

He could already feel his skin crawl. The vague

memories of incarceration in Rikers came flooding back in. The clanging of jail cells, the noise of rowdy inmates and the bleak future of a life behind bars ate away at his mind.

The strangest part about the prison was that the outer section had rooms that doubled as sleeping quarters for the guards. With only twelve doing the rounds, when would they have time to sleep? He shook his head as he passed by the bunk beds covered in green blankets.

He was led into a shower room where he was told to strip so they could make sure he wasn't attempting to bring in any weapons or illegal items like drugs. Why they bothered to do that was beyond him. Drugs and weapons were notorious in USA prisons but in a third world country, and after what Mario had told him, was it worth going to all the effort of a strip search?

"And the rest," a guard said motioning to his underpants.

Two guards stood there as he got butt naked and was told to crouch down and cough. They handed back his clothes and told him to get dressed. That was another thing different about Danlí Prison. They didn't issue prison clothes. No orange garb. No number. Inmates wore regular clothes. Jack went in with the clothes on his back.

No blankets were given.

No toothbrush, toothpaste or any of the typical packages were handed out upon entry.

The next thing on the agenda was a haircut. He slumped down in a chair before a mirror and a guy who looked like he had trouble cutting his lawn strolled up and picked up a trimmer and tore into his thick head of hair. Large chunks of it drifted to the floor leaving him with nothing more than a buzz cut.

Immediately after he was led into an office area where he was fingerprinted, and they made him hold up a decaying piece of wood that had white paint peeling off it and paper numbers stuck to the front. A quick snapshot and he was hustled back out, heading for hell itself.

Twelve - Lion's Den

Beyond the bars of the holding cell, tattooed faces of hardened criminals in for rape, murder and all manner of atrocities stared on, showing little emotion. Some wolf whistled, others pressed against the bars and gyrated and licked their lips. The guards would not venture beyond that point, at least for now. Jack was informed that the general coordinator, named Chepe, would take over from there. Jack nodded, and continued to soak in the nightmare before him.

Guards retreated and locked themselves out leaving Jack alone to wait for the coordinators. It seemed like purgatory. The coordinators were convicts put in charge of the other prisoners. They didn't look any different to them. They were easy to spot, as they were the only ones carrying short wooden batons. The smell that wafted through the bars was like a back alley in Soho. It reeked of grime.

None of this would have been allowed in the USA, it would have been a human rights violation, but here, where the government didn't give two shits, it was normal.

Through the bars, men sat in a line watching others parade past them like cattle. No one seemed to be involved in any activities from what he could see. They looked back at him, a collection of lost souls fearful, unsure, angry and bitter. His eyes drifted around, hoping to see the face of his brother.

Noah was nowhere to be seen.

When Chepe emerged, he wasn't an imposing man. Short in stature, stocky with an expression on his face that made it clear he was in charge, he ambled up to the gate with all the confidence of a lion. Either side were two coordinators with batons. From the moment the iron bars creaked open and Jack was told to enter, the jeering got louder. It was the norm. Prison was a breeding ground for boredom. He was fresh meat. Some would want to challenge him, others fuck him. He had to have eyes in the back of his head from here on out.

With no translator, he had to rely on the little Spanish he knew as none of them seemed to respond to English. If they knew the language, they weren't interested in answering. They led him through the maze of bartolinas, small aqua-colored shanties that acted as cells. They weren't the typical housing for inmates he'd seen. More like cramped housing units with prison bars for doors. In fact, the inside of the prison grounds looked like a small village. As Jack passed by several inmates, he noticed one was holding a knife; a block down from him, someone covered up the front of his abdomen to hide a gun. How the hell did they get that in here? The knife he could understand. That occurred often in Rikers but a gun?

"Go in here for a strip search."

"I've already been searched."

"It's for security."

Those inside the compound didn't rely on the guards doing their job. They treated each inmate just as if he had stepped in there for the first time and never been checked.

Once again, Jack went through the humiliation of unclothing in front of two Hondurans.

After the search was completed and they were satisfied that he wasn't sneaking a gun or knife up his ass, Jack was led back to a room where Chepe was waiting. He sat on the edge of his bed drinking yellow fluid from a plastic bottle. Jack didn't even want to ask what it was. His eyes looked wired and in the cramped cell, Jack saw why so many lost their minds.

He took his time finishing his drink before he picked up a pad of paper and pencil and walked around Jack, studying him the way a wild animal might observe its prey before supper.

"What crime did you commit?"

"I didn't."

He smirked and nudged one of his coordinators who snickered. Every inmate believed they were innocent, so he asked again.

"Murder," Jack replied.

His eyebrows rose. Jack had to wonder if they were

assessing the threat level.

He tapped Jack on the shoulder and told him to kneel before him.

"Kneel?"

He got this look in his eye that made it clear that questioning what he ordered was a sure way ticket to an early grave. Reluctantly Jack dropped to one knee. Chepe perched on the edge of his bed and spewed off the rules.

"There is a system in this place. You follow it, things will go well. You don't…" He didn't have to finish what he was saying. Jack nodded. "The men behind you and myself coordinate with the guards outside. If they tell you to do anything, you are to do it. No questions. You understand?"

He nodded.

"Now you're probably wondering where you will sleep. It's simple. If you have money, you can buy a bed if one is available. If you have none, then you will sleep on the ground."

Hell, the place was worse than regular prison. At least

in the U.S. an inmate was assigned a bed, blankets and mattress. Not here. It would cost him one hundred and forty dollars to get a bed without a mattress. It was made crystal-clear that there were many who didn't have a bed. It was a luxury. Overcrowding meant they could be selective. There was a social system to the place. The poor got the shit end of the stick while those who could muster up the green would thrive. Jack didn't have a penny to his name, at least while he was in here.

It was explained that while the coordinators and the guards would try to prevent attacks, if a fight broke out, there was no guarantee they could intervene in time.

After being given a full rundown of the house rules, which pretty much said he was their bitch, he was taken across the courtyard to the cell that would be his abode. Unlike Rikers there were no different levels. The prison was nothing more than a series of shacks with tin roofs, concrete walls and iron bars. Narrowed eyes glared at him as he walked past a line of men. Someone tossed something at him. He didn't see what it was but he felt it strike the back of his head. Laughter erupted. One coordinator pointed a stick but the crowd didn't seem intimidated. Several bald men scoffed and returned to smoking their cigarettes.

"You will stay in C#31."

Jack expected to find one small room with a bunk bed and another disgruntled prisoner, instead he entered a darkened corridor barely wide enough for a man to squeeze through. Either side of him were wooden bunk beds covered by patterned drapes for privacy. The inside was no bigger than a small kitchen. The one he was in was designed for eight but twenty-three men were housed in there.

The smell of bad body odor stung his nostrils, the ground was cold and hard and the walls covered in a thick turquoise paint that had deteriorated and peeled back. Jack was introduced to Ernesto, his cell coordinator. He was a young man, wiry with a bald head, and small spectacles. His clothes hung from his shoulders the way cloth might from a hanger. He greeted Jack with a weak but warm handshake, which was a first. So far all he'd encountered was hostile glares and jeers.

"What is your name?"

"Jack."

"Do you have a bucket?"

"No."

"Get one, as it will be used for showering outside."

"What about a mattress?"

"Buy one."

Jack shook his head. A few of the men smirked. He must have had the same deer in the headlights look that every newbie got, except he wasn't new to being a caged animal. Though this would take some getting used to.

"I have no money," Jack said.

"Then you will have to earn what you need through tasks I will assign to you. Come with me."

He led Jack through another narrow passage to a stone bath, if it could even be called that. It was nothing more than a hole in the ground filled with water.

"You will collect water for those in the cell. Guillermo

will show you where to get it."

Jack nodded and he was handed a bucket.

He exited the claustrophobic dwelling with Guillermo who was grinning from ear to ear and headed over to a trough in the center of the grounds. As Jack scooped water, Guillermo loosened up.

"You from America, yes?"

His English was quite good. Guillermo reminded Jack of a tweaker. He kept bouncing around and eyeing the others in a nervous, almost paranoid state. He was a small, pudgy-looking fella with a cleft lip. He had a full head of dark hair, and wore his shirt open to expose a medallion.

"I am."

"You remind me of another."

Jack stopped what he was doing and put the bucket down. He wished he had a photo to show him but everything had been stripped from him. They took what little personal belongings he had, that included the photo Liz had given him. Still, how many Americans could there have been in that prison? "Another American?"

He nodded.

"Can you take me to him?"

He looked down at the ground and then off towards the guards near the gate. He sucked in his lips and scratched the side of his neck. He looked nervous. Jack scanned the area. The eyes of many were on them. "Just collect the water. We'll speak later."

Thirteen - Trouble In Paradise

Lugging buckets of cold water back and forth from the trough continued for what felt like an hour before Ernesto changed things up and had Jack mop up the toilet floor. A few shakes of powdered bleach and a drop of water and he was a handed a mop and told to get to it. All the while Jack's mind was occupied by the thought of Noah. Guillermo had disappeared leaving him wondering if he had even understood him. Perhaps he was thinking about another American.

The chores continued for another hour, some of which involved dumping a bucket of soiled tissues into a garbage can out in the courtyard because there was no running water being used in the toilets. The water gathered would be used for showers and flushing the shit away.

Jack winced as he got close to the stench-filled can overflowing with human waste. Flies buzzed around it, and some of the contents had spilled over and was running down the side. He gagged.

It was unreal. U.S. jails didn't even come close to the substandard conditions they had to endure.

After spending the better part of the first few hours working like a slave, Jack ventured out into the courtyard to see if he could find Noah. Some men were playing soccer, others lifting weights but most were just milling around. He felt under the watchful eye of the guards in the towers but it wasn't them he felt threatened by; it was the groups of dubious-looking characters staring his way. Inside the compound the atmosphere felt like a ticking time bomb. At any second it could explode and a fight would break out. They were treated worse than caged zoo animals.

It didn't matter where he went inside the compound, he couldn't find Noah. He assumed he was in one of the cells. He'd already been warned not to enter any without an invitation, otherwise it would be seen as a threat. He would have to wait. It would soon be time to eat and then he'd spot him.

Time seemed to stand still.

Without a bed to sleep on, he had to linger outside. All of it brought back memories of being a kid in school. Everyone eyed each other with a sense of distrust. Jack took in the sight of the sixteen-foot walls with barbed wire along the top. He was already thinking about how to break out. Whether Noah was inside or not, he was getting the hell out of here the first chance he got.

Over the course of the next few hours Guillermo was nowhere to be seen. Jack returned to the cell several times and he wasn't around. He asked and the lack of response made it clear he wasn't welcome.

Now whether he was annoying them with his constant questions or they wanted to wear him down, Ernesto decided to have Jack assist him with preparing the food. Food was a luxury in this place. According to Ernesto, when they weren't eating a small amount of rice and a boiled egg, they caught rats and ate them. It was hard to believe but Jack had seen it. At first, he thought the guy was gutting a bird but when he got a little closer he realized it was a rat.

"They don't give us much to eat here. What little they have is meant to feed two hundred and forty not seven hundred men."

"But you eat rats?"

"Some do. I haven't had to but then I've been here a long time and earned the right to larger portions."

By larger portions he meant two eggs instead of one a day, and one more scoop of rice. Even the coordinators weren't given special treatment. Ernesto led him to a section in the east wing where they were unloading vegetables. Very rarely did they see chicken in the prison, and when it arrived it was a donation from some missionary organization. Jack had to wonder if it was the same one that Noah was associated with.

"Have you seen Guillermo?"

"He's busy dealing with tomorrow's fight."

"Fight?"

He smirked but didn't elaborate. When they arrived in the section assigned for cooking it was unlike anything he'd seen before. There was no kitchen, so to speak, though they had a stove and microwave. Both were fried to a crisp.

"What happened there?"

"Destroyed in the riot."

"So how do you cook?"

He pointed to a large steel pot on top of a pile of bricks. Beneath it were chunks of blackened wood. Flames licked up the sides scorching it black. A lone man chopped up more wood.

"Who's that?"

"Rico."

"What's he in for?"

"Murder."

"And they gave him an axe?"

Ernesto laughed. "He's a changed man."

"I hope so," Jack muttered as he lugged large burlap bags full of vegetables from a truck over to the preparation area. A table had been set up and several men were chopping up onions, carrots, potatoes, cabbages and the smallest amount of chicken. There was no way in hell that would feed all of them. Perhaps that's why the guy he'd witnessed earlier butchered that rat.

"How many times do we eat?"

"Three times."

Jack gazed around at the men chopping veggies. All of them had knives and from the looks of it, no guards were watching. To say he felt uneasy would have been an understatement. Jack scanned the area behind him, watching where the men walked.

As they continued to prepare the food, they talked among themselves. Jack asked them how they had wound up in prison. The inmates were more than willing to share their stories. All were very remorseful and wished they could have made a better choice. It was the same all over the world. In Jack's time in Rikers he had heard every kind of sob story for horrific crimes. Society painted them all in a bad light and he agreed, some should never get out, but it was the youngsters, the ones who had been led astray by gangs, that he felt for — he knew that world all too well. People were responsible for the decisions they made in life but all of society was responsible for how they treated each other. He'd had that conversation with John Dalton many a time. Dalton had given himself to rescue the runaways, the throwaways and those deemed by the world as the filth of society. Why he did it was still foreign to Jack. Some would have said his faith played a large role, and yet Dalton wasn't what Jack would have called a religious man. Perhaps that's why he liked him. His head was in the heavens but his feet fixed on the ground. Maybe that's why he could relate to people and help those on Skid Row.

The sound of a truck drawing near caught Jack's attention. He glanced to his side. Through the fence he saw another handful of prisoners being brought in.

"How many arrive each day?"

"I lost count," Ernesto said. "They come and go."

"But there's already too many."

"They have a way to handle that."

Jack frowned. There was something he wasn't telling

him, an underlying tension to a place full of secrecy. He sliced a cucumber watching intently as they unloaded the next batch of men and marched them inside. Jack noticed that among the six that went inside, one of them was an American-looking guy.

"Ernesto, Guillermo said there is another American in here, is that right?"

He nodded.

"Do you know where I can find him?"

"Don't get involved. Keep your head down. Say nothing. You see nothing. You say nothing. The fewer questions you ask, the better for you."

"I need to know."

Ernesto's eyes went from the knife in Jack's hand to him. "He's three blocks down from us but don't go in there. I'm warning you."

Jack went to ask another question but Ernesto refused to answer as guards made their way along the outside of the perimeter to make sure that everything was okay. There was a gate a few yards away. In the event someone got stabbed, it was possible they would venture in, though it was becoming clear that the inmates governed each other. The coordinators were meant to be the first line of defense against unruly inmates but with so few of them and only batons for weapons, how was that considered protection?

After the food was prepared, it was wheeled into an area where the inmates could collect a small amount before retreating to perching like birds on lower walls. Inmates seemed to favor the walls, which offered a small amount of protection from attacks from behind while giving them a bird's-eye view of the compound.

Three scoops with a plastic spoon and Jack's meal was over. It was not enough to feed a bird. No wonder most of them look malnourished. After supper Jack wandered into the courtyard to where people were working out. Weights were nothing more than concrete on the end of iron bars. Several muscle heads walked around flexing their guns and establishing their territory. That's when Jack noticed one of them making a gesture towards the newcomers entering on the north side of the prison. Like wolves in a pack, they made their way across the yard. One of them stood out — a bald ape-like man, with a large spiderweb tattoo on the back of his head. He removed his shirt and one man beside him took it. On his back was a large tattoo of an upside-down cross. The guy was ripped. The curious pack of men waited until the guards had retreated before moving in on the newcomers who looked overwhelmed by the amount of interest they were getting.

That's when the guy struck. He rushed over to one newcomer and before anyone knew what had happened, stabbed him three times in the side and he dropped to the ground. It was precise, fast and the entire thing was over before guards could even figure out what had happened. He slipped back into the crowd and his pal handed back his shirt.

Now perhaps that would have been the end of that, but Jack was still staring as he returned to pump iron. He scowled a little as if expecting Jack to turn away but he didn't. Whether that was a mistake or not, he would soon find out.

Fourteen - Nightmares

As darkness fell over the compound, Jack settled in for what would be one of the most uncomfortable nights of his life. At nine o'clock two guards on the outside of the prison entered to lock up the bartolinas. The routine was the same every night. Chepe and the coordinators worked with the guards to ensure that everyone was inside their cell. Once the iron door was closed, they asked how many were inside.

"Twenty-three," Ernesto said from inside. The guard went on his way and silence fell over the place. Jack took his place on the hard concrete floor while all the others rested on mattresses. Two men shared a small space beneath a bed. How they managed to fit under there was a mystery. Arms and legs stuck out.

Jack had no pillow, no blanket, and nothing to put between him and the hard ground. He leaned his back against the wall and sat there while others snored.

Nineteen years? There was no way in hell he could endure nineteen days in here. He could understand why many men took their lives. No one cared. It was one less body to feed.

Every now and again he would hear someone sob. It was hard to tell if it was coming from one of those in the cell he was in or farther down. Alone with his thoughts he found comfort in remembering the good times with Isabel. He closed his eyes and envisioned a day in the summer with her. Waking up in a warm bed, running his hands over her soft skin and making love. He could hear the swell of the ocean waves, the sound of the birds and for a few minutes he was lost in the past until he heard a jail cell open, men speaking in Spanish and then an American's voice.

"No. No! Get away!"

Jack went to get up and he felt a hand touch his shoulder. "Leave it."

It was Ernesto. But he couldn't. The screams were bloodcurdling. Were they the screams of his brother? He had to know. Jack crossed over to the iron bars and gazed out. It was hard to see anything except the silhouette of figures a few doors down.

"Make it quick," a guard said standing watch. A cigarette was lit and in the glow of the flame he saw the bald man with the spiderweb tattoo enter a cell and close the door behind him. What took place over the next ten minutes, Jack could only imagine. Rape occurred in prisons, though usually in the showers or when inmates were singled out but this was happening while a guard stood by.

He could hear the grunting of a man, and the scream of another. Jack returned to his place on the cold ground, it felt even colder than before. He stared down and watched a cockroach rush by only to see one inmate scoop it up at the last second and pop it into his mouth.

No one was safe.

The high-pitched wailing of the American continued for what felt like half an hour until it stopped. Jack's eyes were closed when something landed on his lap. He glanced down to find a blanket. He looked up to see Guillermo in a top bunk smiling. He gave a nod of appreciation and placed it beneath him. The temperature felt like 88 degrees inside, so staying warm wasn't the issue.

That night Jack got little sleep. When he did, his mind replayed the events of the day, except instead of the stranger getting shanked, it was him. Like having an out-of-body experience, he loomed over his dead body as blood drained away like a river and rats feasted upon his flesh.

When his eyelids cracked open, it was Ernesto.

"Wake up. Time for breakfast."

Jack rose and arched his back. All the muscles in his body ached. Tension had set into his neck. He handed back the blanket to Guillermo and thanked him. Even in the bowels of hell there was kindness to be found.

As they streamed out into the blazing sunshine, Jack put up his forearm to block the glare. He looked to his left and right and watched the downtrodden inmates trudge towards to the area assigned for eating.

"Guillermo," Jack nodded. "That cell down there, is that where the American is?"

He nodded and walked on. Jack stood there for a moment until a coordinator told him to get moving. As he got in line he saw the cell door open and a beaten, bruised American stumbled out. His heart sank. It wasn't Noah. The man could barely walk as he was guided towards the line. Further down, the bald man came into view with a smile on his face. His goons were beside him.

"Guillermo, who is that?"

"Pueblo."

"The American. That's not the man I'm looking for."

He shrugged and continued to shuffle forward because the coordinators were tapping inmates on the arm to keep the line flowing. Slowly but surely, he noticed Pueblo walk over to the American and the man cowered back. They laughed and continued on, only to catch Jack's eye. It was the second time, however this time Pueblo didn't just glare, he strolled up and squeezed in line behind Jack.

As the line came to a halt while inmates were being served what slop they had on the menu, Pueblo leaned in and whispered into Jack's ear.

"You're mine."

Now whether it was the need to establish a line in the sand, or anger for what he'd done to one of his own people, or that the American wasn't Noah and he was no closer to finding him, but Jack reacted.

A swift elbow backwards into Pueblo's solar plexus and a backhand to the face sent him reeling back. Inmates jeered as Pueblo rushed Jack and they hit the dirt. Jack reared back his head and headbutted him on the ground, and was about to strangle him when several hard batons rained down on his back. One struck him on the side of the ear and it was like being hit with a steel rod. A shot of pain, a blur of boots and he was hauled up by three coordinators while the others held back Pueblo. His nose was bleeding and he was spitting profanity as Jack was hauled away.

Punishment was swift.

A few of Chepe's men handed Jack over to the guards who then took him to an isolated area of the compound. He knew what was coming. He'd experienced it in Rikers. The question was would solitary confinement be the same?

He was led down a series of stone steps, along a darkened corridor until they reached a steel door. There were several, four rooms in total that looked the same. The noise of the violent offenders banging on them echoed off the crumbling stone walls.

Once thrown inside, Jack took in the sight of his cell. It smelled dank and musty. There was hardly any paint on the walls, a single bed frame was in the middle minus a mattress. There were no blankets or pillows and a lone toilet not attached to any plumbing was off to his right. The ceiling was arched and in the center was a shaft of daylight flooding in through a small opening half his size. It was barred. The door slammed behind him and he shouted back.

"Now you give me a bed?"

Fifteen - The Hole

There was no way of knowing when they would release him. Solitary confinement was the worst place to be, no matter what prison you were in. In Rikers, Jack had been confined in a cell for twenty-three hours with only one hour a day allotted for exercise. There were inmates who had been confined for up to eight years in solitary. Never seeing another human being except a guard. Every inmate handled it differently. Some were so desperate for outside contact they hallucinated, interpreted the rush of wind through vents as whispers or resorted to feeding spiders, bugs.

Most couldn't handle the silence, or the noise of others raging against being locked up for so long. Seconds felt like minutes, minutes like hours, and hours like days. Routine would set in and Jack recalled waking up each day and cleaning his cell just to kill the hours. But here? There was nothing to clean. No water to clean with. It was worse than caging an animal. In fact, even animals wouldn't get treated like this.

Though used by the system to discipline wrongdoers, it rarely corrected their behavior. Segregation led to mental problems. Hypersensitivity to stimuli, hallucinations, hate-filled fantasies, rage, weight loss, self-mutilation and suicidal thoughts.

Confinement didn't calm the rage, it only intensified it, causing men to become a worse version of themselves. Slumped on the ground, Jack beat his knuckles against the floor as rage rose in his chest. He got up and slammed his fist against the door.

There was no response.

He paced, dropped and did a few push-ups just to get the blood flowing.

As the hours drifted, morning turned into afternoon and the sun waned, he heard someone approach the door. A slat was opened at the bottom and food on a tray was slid inside. An apple, a few carrots and the head of a rat. He scoffed it all down except the rat's head.

From beyond the wall he could hear others. A man speaking in Spanish, praying over and over for God to deliver him and yet no one would save him now. The cries of another man pleading with the guards to let him out. How long had he been in there?

Solitary. He recalled it all too well. In the first few days an inmate might kick back against the punishment or do the opposite and remain calm hoping to be let out but as the days turned into weeks they would go through a whole range of emotions. Guilt, rage, desperation, hate, denial and acceptance.

Light turned into darkness and Jack glanced at the wire-framed bed. He sat on the edge and leaned back on the exposed steel springs. Each one dug into his flesh but the alternative of lying on the damp, cold ground was even worse.

Slowly but surely Jack could feel himself unraveling as the days continued to roll by. From outside his cell he could hear familiar voices and sounds. Some kicking at their doors, others beating their fists or heads against the wall. His knuckles were already raw and bloody from unleashing his anger on the door two days prior.

It was hard to believe it had come to this.

"Hello!" Jack called out hoping that the other inmates could hear him. Another one replied in Spanish telling him to shut his mouth. He continued regardless. That's when he heard a reply. It was barely audible but it was American.

"Noah?"

There was silence, he asked again. "Is that you, Noah?"

He'd all but given up hope that Noah was incarcerated here. For a while he had thought perhaps he was dead, or Liz had been told the wrong information. But when the words came back, he couldn't have been any more relieved.

"Who are you?"

"Noah Matthews, is that you?"

"Yeah. Who are you?"

Jack chuckled a little and rested his head against the wall. He was tired, hungry and at the end of his rope.

Days of being locked inside that hole had already broken him wide open like tearing the scab off an old wound.

"Hello brother!"

There was no reply.

Then, in an almost skeptical tone the voice drifted back.

"Brother? Who are you?" he demanded to know.

"Jack Winchester."

"Jack? Jack?"

His voice got stronger and he heard him beating on his cell.

"The one and only."

"What the hell are you doing in here?"

Jack turned around and slumped down against the door with his back turned towards it. He rocked his head back and rested it.

"Would you believe me if I said I was here to break you out?"

A small laugh, then even harder. It was infectious as Jack soon joined in. Tiredness overtook and he saw the amusing side to it all.

"How's that working out?" Noah asked.

"I'll keep you posted."

He snorted. It was good to hear his voice even though he hadn't ever met him in person. Though they were locked up behind thick metal, enclosed within hard stone, hearing his voice was like a lifeline.

"How's my mother doing?"

"Right about now she is probably bouncing off the walls."

"Sounds like her. Damn. I can't believe you are here."

"How long you been down here?" Jack asked.

"A week. Some asshole thought he would become my bunk buddy. I nipped that idea in the bud."

Jack laughed. "What, you beat him?"

There was hesitation in his voice, perhaps guilt. "Killed him."

There was silence for a while.

"Did you come in alone?"

"No, they brought me and Henry in."

"The other American."

"Yeah, you seen him?"

Jack didn't reply.

"Henry's a friend of mine."

The sound of the American man's cries, and the images of him the next morning flooded Jack's mind. The horrors of prison life could break a man within days. Even those who considered themselves tough would buckle under the strain.

"Yeah, he's still alive."

"Good, I thought he would end up the same as me."

It was far worse. There were many downsides to confinement, safety wasn't one of them. Though Jack had to wonder how safe they were here after a guard had let Pueblo into Henry's cell.

No sooner had the conversation started than he heard keys jangling and boots pounding the ground. A key was inserted into the lock of his door, it clunked and an officer beckoned for him to step out.

"Is that it?"

"You've got a visitor."

"A visitor?"

They strong-armed him out. As he passed by the cell that housed his brother, Noah called out to him. "Jack? Jack?"

"It's okay, I'll be back."

He couldn't be sure about that, but in solitary, hope of getting out was the only thing that kept people alive. They marched Jack up the narrow staircase that led him back out into the courtyard. A bright morning sun blinded him. He squinted. Though the cell had light, it was hardly anything and he had sat in the shadows for far too long. His eyes stung and his mouth felt parched.

Walking through the courtyard, he got a few claps from the inmates while others jeered. He saw Ernesto and Chepe, and as he rounded the corner he spotted Pueblo leaning back against a wall. His eyes narrowed and he made a gesture with his finger across his throat to indicate what he would do. Jack winked at him to piss him off.

Guiding him out of the compound with his wrists in

cuffs, he was led towards a large building in the outer perimeter. As he got closer he recognized the number plate on one vehicle. It had been parked outside Lázaro's home.

Buzzed in through several doors, he stood before Lázaro. He had his back turned and was gazing out the window. It overlooked the prison compound. He had his hands locked behind his back and was wearing a gray suit. When he turned, he waved off the guard and they closed the door.

"Take a seat."

"I'll stand if that's okay."

"Suit yourself."

Before saying anything, he went over to a small table and poured himself out a drink of coffee.

"Would you like one?"

"I'll pass."

He grinned a little as he filled his cup and the aroma of fresh coffee beans filled the air. Not that he wouldn't have killed for a cup of coffee but the dynamics between the two of them had changed. No longer was he trying to bargain.

"You must excuse the delay in me getting to speak with you. I've had a lot on my plate."

"Yeah, making room for that hundred thousand dollars must be real hard."

He snorted. "About that. It's unfortunate, I thought we could reach an agreement but fate has a strange sense of humor."

"Where is the money?"

"Oh, let's not discuss that. Who cares about the money? That's not of concern to you, is it?"

Jack didn't reply.

He continued. "Getting out of here is what matters, right?"

Jack gave a nod.

"I hear you landed yourself in solitary for fighting. You fight well, do you?"

Where was he going with this? "Let me out of these cuffs and I'll demonstrate."

His lip curled up while he stirred his coffee and took a seat.

"The way I see it. You have a lengthy sentence ahead of you, Jack. The life expectancy of someone in Danlí is low. So you have a few options. You can continue with the attitude and I can have my man outside take you right back to solitary, where I believe your brother is. How is he?"

Jack ground his teeth.

"What do you want?"

"What does anyone want, Jack?" He got up and walked over to the window and sipped at his coffee. "All those men down there are just waiting to explode or implode. It will happen. It always does. The last riot we had was kicked off by the smallest thing. Would you like to know what it was?"

"A hair in someone's food?" Jack muttered.

"Close. No, before we instituted coordinators, there were several people vying for control of the prison. Like in any village, town, city or organization there is always one that wants to rule over others. The man in charge at the time raped a visitor of another prisoner. This caused a massive riot, over eight people died and by the time it was over, Luis the man who had committed that foul act was strung up and his heart was torn from his chest and fed to the dogs. They then burned the others involved and their bodies were found in various places throughout the courtyard."

"And?" Jack asked.

"The government doesn't and won't pay for more guards because in their eyes, it's a waste. I agree. The more you hire, the more people will die. But I found a solution. Men have all this pent-up frustration. At least those inside the walls do. Unless they have a means to unleash that, it bottles up and eventually boils over. So I came up with a way to keep everyone calm and happy. The inmates regulate each other, while the few guards we have ensure that they don't escape the perimeter."

"Twelve people?"

"It's not about numbers, Jack. I used to think it was.

It's about leverage. Why don't those prisoners push back? Why don't they fight the guards like they did in that riot? Simple. They know we can remove privileges and make their life hard when they come up for their parole hearing."

"So you managed to save some money. Good for you," Jack said with an edge to his voice.

Lázaro smiled and sipped at his coffee. "That's not all. Men with all that pent-up frustration need an outlet but more than that, they need hope. I provide that. Every week, we hold a fight inside the compound. The winner receives time off their sentence, the loser, well... I'm sure you can figure that out."

"So pit the men against each other like dogs."

"We all have a dog inside of us, two to be exact. The good and the bad."

"Spare me the story. I've heard it before."

"Then you know who wins, yes?"

Jack rocked his head back and rolled it around.

"Where are you going with this?" Jack asked growing

impatient with him.

"You want freedom. I can give you that. But without money, you will earn it. I'm sure the coordinators have explained the rules inside the compound. There are no free handouts, everything is earned on a reward system. You have to work for it. But what I am offering you here is a sure way to fast-track yourself and your brother out of Danlí Prison."

"You want us to fight?"

"Not each other. Others."

"And if I win?"

"I reduce your sentence. How many years were you given? Twenty, thirty?"

"Nineteen," Jack muttered. He could feel his blood boiling inside of him. He knew a setup when he saw one.

"So?" Lázaro asked.

"What about my brother?"

"Yeah, that's where it gets a little tricky. He's a good fighter but not an agreeable inmate."

Jack frowned.

"He refused to fight."

"So you placed him in solitary?"

"Just for now, until he comes around. I hoped that you might do that. I mean, I might not get through to him but you could."

Jack stepped back and studied Lázaro.

"And what do you get out of this?"

"A peaceful prison."

"Bullshit."

He smirked and came around his desk and leaned back against it, perched on the edge.

"Do you know how much they pay a warden in Honduras, Jack?"

"A lot by the looks of your home and flashy cars."

"Oh I think you're smart enough to know my salary didn't pay for all of that."

Jack shrugged.

"In the USA. Fifty-eight thousand. Down here. Barely one-tenth of that."

"So you steal from Americans? Is that it?"

"Oh, I'm offended, Jack. That you would think I would do that just for a hundred thousand?"

"Not just for a hundred."

"Perhaps you are smarter than you let on. I have friends that wager money on the fights. But that's neither here nor there. The real question is, how much do you want your freedom?"

Jack eyed him.

"How many fights?"

"You've been given nineteen years? So nineteen fights."

Sixteen - Fight Fire with Fire

Jack made a deal with Lázaro that he would speak with his brother on one condition. That he was released back into general population. Lázaro was hesitant at first to do that but then he agreed. He warned him that if he screwed up, both of them would get thrown back in the hole and he wouldn't be as lenient next time.

After being returned to his cellblock he kind of expected that the shit would hit the fan. Pueblo had eyes on him and now that he was back he'd have to keep a lookout for him. Upon returning to his cell, Ernesto put him back to work collecting water, emptying buckets full of shitty tissues and cleaning floors. While he didn't enjoy it, it kept his mind occupied.

He was filling a bucket when he felt a hand on his back. Jack turned to find Noah.

"I'm guessing I have you to thank for getting me out."

"Don't sing my praises yet," Jack replied, his eyes

narrowed.

Noah shook his hand and patted him on the shoulder. It was the first time he'd seen him beyond the photos. There was some resemblance between them. Though the photos hadn't done him any justice, he was larger in person and had packed on some weight and muscle since.

"You don't look like the same man I saw in the photos."

"Oh she showed you those, did she?"

He nodded. Noah stared around at the other inmates, keeping an eye out for anyone who might attack. There was no respect in prisons — only opportunity. If a man's back was turned they wouldn't think twice about shanking him in the kidneys.

Noah followed him back to his cell. Once he had wrapped up cleaning the floors, they wandered off to have a smoke. Cigarettes were like everything else in there. There was a price but he had worked out an agreement with a guard. What he exchanged was unknown as he told Jack he'd be back in a few minutes. From a distance

Jack observed him talk to a guard beyond the gate, and then he saw him slip Noah a packet of cigarettes and matches. There was something more to Noah that his mother hadn't shared. She gave him the impression he was a clean-cut guy who was in the wrong place at the wrong time. Was that true?

They strolled to the far end of the courtyard and he offered Jack a cigarette, they lit up and watched a crowd of inmates kicking a ball around.

"So how do you think they got drugs into your bag?" Jack asked.

Noah blew out smoke looking all relaxed. It was unusual to see someone new to prison life looking as though they had spent the better part of ten years in there.

"They didn't," he said.

Jack frowned. "Run that by me again."

"No one snuck drugs into my bag. Those were mine."

"What?"

He snorted. "Oh right, mother passed on the version I

gave her."

He gripped the bridge of his nose feeling a tension headache coming on. "Are you telling me that what landed you in here was of your own accord?"

"It was a mistake. A misunderstanding. There was a mix-up in shift changes and the guy who was paid to look the other way wasn't on shift. And being as the next one hadn't been paid, well, I wound up here."

Jack dropped the cigarette and crushed it beneath his boot.

"You were taking drugs?"

"Not taking, I'm not that stupid. Selling. It's a lucrative business."

Jack grabbed a hold of him by the collar and slammed him up against the wall, he tried to push back but it was useless, Jack was stronger.

"She thought you were set up."

"I was. Nothing I told her was a lie, Jack. I was set up by the man I bought drugs from. He knew about the shift change. He was disgruntled because I owed him money. I bent the truth a little. I'm sure you've done that from time to time."

Through gritted teeth Jack spoke. He was seething. "I came down here to get your ass out of prison. I risked life and limb only to end up here and lose a hundred grand."

"I didn't ask her to get me out."

"But you knew she would try."

"She's my mother."

Jack shook his head and released his grip. It was one thing to have ended up in prison because someone had planted drugs, quite another to know the drugs were bought by Noah and he'd planned to sneak them back into the USA for distribution.

He was fuming.

Right then Chepe and several of the coordinators shouted for the inmates to line up. Jack cast a glance over his shoulder, glared at his brother and joined the line. He saw Henry emerge from a building. His eyes widened when he caught sight of Noah. It was the small things that kept them sane.

"Listen up, a forest fire has started and like usual we are the ones being called in to assist. Anyone who wants to help, line up."

It was a common procedure in the United States. Battling raging wildfires was handled by state fire services but a third of them were prisoners. It gave inmates a way to earn money and get an early release by doing an exhausting, grimy and dangerous job. They didn't get paid much, it was about $2 an hour, less down in Honduras. It wasn't mandatory but by the looks of how many were lined up, everyone down here was taking full of advantage of it.

As they streamed out, each of them was assigned a number and told to get into a line that corresponded to that number. Jack glanced off to his side and saw Pueblo glaring at him. From there, they were taken in trucks from the compound by armed guards to a local fire service and equipped with the essentials, such as orange overalls, backpacks, construction hats and tools.

Jack had always thought it was a little insane to send

out violent criminals to fight fires alongside the public. They might not have given them a chainsaw but they were all given hoes and rakes. Those were deadly weapons in the hands of a prisoner.

A firefighter dressed in black stepped in front of them all and shouted in Spanish.

"Listen up, my name is Leonel Silver. We don't have time to deal with any issues today. You want to act like a firefighter, I will treat you like one, if you want to act like a prisoner, I will treat you like one. I do both well. You decide." He stopped for a second and turned to another firefighter and gave him some instructions. "There is a forest fire that is threatening the main water sources in the region. This will be a long day, so let's get started."

Though several armed guards went with the crew of sixty that left that day, it was Chepe and coordinators who appeared to be keeping everyone in line.

Everyone piled into the back of multiple red trucks. There was enough room in each for up to about ten people but they packed in close to twenty. Pueblo wasn't inside his truck otherwise he figured he'd try something.

The truck rumbled to life and peeled away. Men stared at the floor. It was hot, sweaty and the worst conditions possible, and yet it was better than being stuck inside those walls. Along the way, Noah looked over at Jack and though he was on the other side of the truck, he could tell that the dynamics between them had changed. It wasn't just the fact he'd lied to their mother that bothered him. It was that he had tried to help someone who he thought had been imprisoned falsely. There was nothing false about it. And yet now Liz was relying on him to get Noah out. The only way out was attempting to escape over a wall or fighting. Neither appealed to him.

They flooded out of the back of the trucks upon reaching the destination, which was over an hour away. Leonel Silver barked out orders.

"Someone grab the hose and fittings. You guys over there get in line and make your way up."

It was a long trek up a road that wound its way around the forest. They could already hear the wood crackling in the distance farther up the mountain. There was a slight breeze. The smell of smoke permeated the air.

Jack kept his eyes peeled for trouble. It wasn't just prisoners wielding tools that bothered him but all the trees that had been charred and might collapse at any moment. He heard a helicopter circling overhead, and then it felt like it was raining for a minute as droplets of water fell from above.

"Guys, to contain the fire we will create a line around it, now get started."

The inmates fell in and scraped at the earth to form a barrier line of dirt. It was called a firebreak. The whole point of it was to remove deadwood and undergrowth so that all that remained was soil. This naturally occurred when there was a river, lake or canyon but in the forest, it had to be man-made.

After about twenty minutes, Chepe came along and yelled at the inmates. "Hey, we are not gardening here. Put your back into it."

Jack watched as the coordinators wandered up and

down the line. There were too many inmates to watch all of them at the same time and by the looks Pueblo was throwing Jack's way, he kind of figured shit was about to kick off.

Jack tightened his grip on the rake and readied himself.

What he didn't expect was what happened next.

Henry broke line and charged towards Pueblo but was quickly taken out of commission by one of Pueblo's guys who swung his hoe and caught him on the side of the head. Henry hit the dirt on the steep slope and rolled down. That only incited Noah. He went to react but Jack grabbed his arm.

"Wait!"

Noah looked back at him and then noticed Chepe rushing over, screaming at the men in Spanish. They backed off and he wanted to know what happened. It had occurred so fast, and he'd been looking the other way, that it was hard to tell who had struck first. All he could see was that someone had assaulted Henry. Chepe gestured to a few men to collect him. Henry was groaning a quarter of the way down the slope. A tree had broken his fall and probably a few ribs.

"That bastard," Noah muttered.

Pueblo looked over at Jack and grinned. It wasn't over. He'd get what was coming to him but they had to be smart about it. Barreling in there the way Henry had, all full of emotion over being raped, would not cut it. These guys were used to having a target on their backs. And under the watchful eye of Chepe and the firefighters, it wasn't the place to start a riot.

The men hauled Henry back to the top of the steep incline and carried him off to get medical attention. Chepe went down the line asking if anyone saw what happened. No one said a word. That's just how it worked inside. It wasn't worth it.

But Jack wouldn't stand by. He wanted to make it damn clear he wasn't scared of Pueblo. He gestured to Chepe and he came over. Jack muttered in his ear while looking at Pueblo. Out of earshot, he wasn't telling him that Pueblo's men were to blame, only that he wanted to get himself a drink but he wanted it to appear as though he was snitching on him.

At least that way he might draw the attention away from Henry, as no doubt he would be punished twice as hard for his attempt on Pueblo's life.

As the day passed and the sun waned, they were all given a fifteen-minute break. Guys tossed down their backpacks and leaned back on them, staring out across the valley. Some knocked back water or chewed on apples that had been handed out. There was a sense of accomplishment in knowing they had saved people's homes, and yet Jack could feel the tension brewing.

"See them over there," Noah said leaning on his side while chewing. He was gesturing to Chepe and the firefighters who would occasionally disappear down the line of men. "I've been timing it, we have maybe a three-minute window, four tops. You up for it?"

"Don't be stupid, you'll be shot before you even make it a few yards."

"Hell, if we stay in here any longer we will die anyway."

"Maybe not," Jack said. "I spoke with the warden today about fighting."

"Fighting? Freedom? Oh, that bullshit? It's what he tells the inmates to get them to fight."

"So why did you stop?"

"Because I'm not into killing men."

"What?"

"Oh, he left that part out, did he?" He smirked and took another large bite of the red apple. "What do you think happens to the loser?"

"He wouldn't dare."

"Wouldn't he? Who will tell? Hell, people die inside Danlí every day, and there are always new ones coming in. How else do you think they handle the overcrowded prisons down here? It' s not like the UN Human Rights Council will step in. Down here, Jack, no one cares unless you have money." He rubbed his finger and thumb together.

"Did you fight?" Jack asked.

"For a while. Two men, the second was an American. A friend of mine. Leland Winters."

He stopped talking and stared down at the ground.

"And?"

"I wouldn't fight him so they gave us a choice. Fight or get thrown in the hole. I didn't want to but we fought and once I had knocked him out, Lázaro wanted me to finish him." He snorted and shook his head before tossing the apple core down the slope and then getting up.

"Did you kill him?"

"No, they tossed me in the hole."

"So what happened to him?"

"Pueblo finished him off."

Noah brushed the dirt from his pants.

"To win a bet?" Jack asked.

He snorted. "You think he drives around in fancy cars and lives in a fine house from the money he gets from betting? Think again. He sells their organs on the black market."

Seventeen - Courtyard Animals

The next morning at breakfast, all the inmates that had helped out were exhausted. The night had passed without incident. Jack had expected Pueblo to show up but Ernesto informed him that rarely did anyone attack the day after hard labor, and with the fights arranged, few needed to put their neck on the line when they could settle it in the cage.

Jack was scooping warm oats into his mouth when he felt a pat on his shoulder. At first, he thought it was his brother. When he turned he found Pueblo. He leaned over and coughed up a wad of phlegm and spat it into his food.

"I will see you tonight."

Jack wanted to react and he would but to do so in that moment would have been premature and earned him a one-way ticket into the hole. Noah however couldn't restrain himself. He leapt up and smashed his metal tray into the face of one of Pueblo's men. Now Jack had no choice. As Pueblo turned to react, Jack swiveled around and smashed him hard in the nuts. As he doubled over in pain, Jack followed through with an uppercut knocking him back into another guy.

That's when all chaos broke out.

The coordinators rushed in to break it up but were swiftly dealt with by other men who had got caught up in the rumble. What started as a fight between two men escalated into an all-out brawl, spreading like wildfire.

Prisoners lashed out at each other with anything they had in their hands.

Over the top of the fence, multiple smoke grenades were fired by guards trying to cause further confusion, but all it did was give inmates cover to beat, stab and even fire a few rounds. Grown men hit the ground at the sound of gunfire while others scrambled for cover as more shots erupted.

Jack was laying into one of Pueblo's men when he felt a baton strike him on the top half of his back, he turned in time to feel it connect with his face. He hit the ground, spitting blood for a few seconds before getting up and trying to figure out where Noah had gone. Everyone was coughing and choking on the smoke. One moment he could see figures ahead of him, the next a knee came out of nowhere and he fell back. Roll, he told himself as a foot came down from above. He swept the leg out and jammed his fist into the throat of one man. All around him was total anarchy. The sound of cursing, boots running, bones cracking and men's cries filled the air. Chairs were being thrown, buckets and anything that wasn't bolted down.

A rapid series of rounds were fired above their heads from multiple places and then the fighting ceased. By the time Jack stumbled out of the smoke, he had taken down four guys.

When the guards had regained order with the help of the coordinators, those who didn't need medical treatment were lined up for another day of hard labor in the mountains.

"This is bullshit," Noah said.

"Just consider yourself lucky that no one saw you, otherwise you would be in the hole."

Noah scowled. "Does it matter? This whole place is a hole. A shit hole. At least down there I can have peace."

Chepe came over and pulled Jack to one side. "You better get a grip on your brother. I had money on the fights that took place today. That little outburst of his is going to cost him."

"Why are you speaking to me? Speak to him," Jack said.

Chepe turned and standing beyond the gate was Lázaro. Chepe didn't have any money on the fights. He was simply passing along a message.

Lázaro sneered and walked away.

* * *

By the time they made it back to the mountains it was almost eleven in the morning. This time they were flown out in a helicopter. As the thump of the rotors beat overhead, Jack looked down at the acres upon acres of burned forest. The sun was beating down and a harsh wind was blowing through the trees bringing with it the smell of burnt wood. With over forty pounds of gear on him, Jack was sweating as he hacked away at the ground for the first hour then spent the next few hours thinning trees.

Some of the fires were 100 feet tall. Now whether the outburst had mellowed everyone out or whether the inmates were exhausted, very little was said by any of them. Everyone got started. The growl of a chainsaw filled the air, along with the thud of axes and rakes scraping the ground. Inmates continued to patrol different areas after a section of fire was put out to make sure it didn't flare up.

"Move out of the way," someone yelled as a falling tree came crashing down and debris flew up in the air. A cry was heard and several men rushed down a steep incline to a man who hadn't moved in time. His arm was stuck under a tree. It was sickening sight. He'd lost it for sure.

Among the insults thrown at each other and the

threats and glares, there were moments when people didn't act like animals. There was something about hard work that made a man feel alive. A sense of accomplishment. That was one of the many reasons the inmates were involved. It was to prepare them for when they were released. The fire chief gave some spiel at the break about how many inmates had been helped over the years and how many of them were now full-fledged firefighters after getting out of prison.

Jack could see the appeal. For many inside the walls of Danlí, they needed a break. Someone to give them a chance at a better life.

"I'm doing it with or without you," Noah said casting his eyes around while scraping at the terrain.

"How?" Jack replied.

"Doesn't matter."

"It will if you have a bullet in your back," Jack said.

"Robert is coming."

Robert shuffled over. He was the other American that Jack had seen enter the prison not long after he arrived.

Another fuck-up who had got caught for stabbing some pimp. He pleaded self-defense but after hearing Noah's lies, Jack didn't believe anyone. There was a saying in prison that no one was guilty. Everyone had an excuse. It was only when they were heading down the green mile to be executed for their crimes that some took responsibility.

"Let's say you make it out of here, how are you going to escape Honduras?"

"Who gives a fuck? I'll figure that out when I get to that hurdle. Right now, I'm getting out of here. You said you came in to get me out. This is our chance, brother."

"No. Use your head."

"Suit yourself."

Jack shook his head.

"What? You think you have a better idea?"

Jack continued to hack away at a tree, thinning out the branches. He coughed as some of the foliage got in his face.

"Far from it. But dodging bullets isn't smart."

"And neither is staying here." Noah slapped him on

the chest. "Look, you know if we don't bounce now, there is only one way we are getting out of here, and that's in a body bag."

Jack contemplated what he said for a second. Not that he hadn't considered escaping. There were no fences, no walls, and few guards in the mountains. But that wasn't what he was worried about. It was trying to escape Honduras.

Another hour passed, then an idea came to him.

"Okay."

"Really?" Noah looked surprised.

"But we do it my way. You follow my lead."

"You got it."

"We wait until the sun goes down, when we get our dinner break."

Noah moved down the line and whispered to Robert. Over the next few hours, Noah looked pleased with himself. Fucking guy would be the death of them all. The only reason he'd agreed was because he knew Lázaro wasn't a man of his word. There was no chance in hell he would let them out after nineteen fights, hell even sixty fights. This was all one big game to him.

When it was time for chow, everyone settled down on their backpacks for dinner. They waited until Chepe and the fire chief were busy discussing work for the next day when they bolted. There was no method to the madness, except to put as much distance between themselves and the crew, and head toward the fire. If they even attempted to descend the mountain, they would run into crew on the road. No one in their right mind would try to follow them into the fire. It was dangerous and the odds of them actually escaping were slim but Jack wouldn't let Noah go alone.

They hadn't even made it a few yards when the guards opened fire. Robert was struck in the back and Noah turned but Jack grabbed him.

"No time, let's go."

Jack's legs screamed in protest as they scaled up the steep incline, using burning trees and the thick smoke as cover. Behind his fogged-up mask, his breathing was

JON MILLS

labored.

"Which way?"

Fire raged around them. Not far behind them they could hear guards yelling. Jack had done a lot of stupid things in his time but this one was right up there. He pointed east and they darted in and out of the trees. Occasionally they would stumble and hit the dirt. Ascending a mountain was tough enough; one wrong footing and they could fall to their deaths. But when the heat of the fire was added into the mix it was almost unbearable.

What made it even more dangerous was that trees were collapsing around them. Every crack and pop of wood put his nerves on edge.

The guards didn't pursue them for long. They didn't earn enough and the firefighters wouldn't come after two hardened criminals. They jogged through the treacherous terrain for what felt like hours, stopping only for a few minutes to catch their breath and take a sip of water from the bottles they brought.

Eventually they made it out of the ring of fire and reached a rocky plateau that overlooked the city. Jack lifted his breathing mask and goggles. Sweat poured off his brow as he wiped it with the back of his forearm.

Noah patted him on the back. "We did it, brother."

Jack shook his head and rolled his eyes. They weren't out of trouble yet.

"What now?" Noah asked.

"Now we pay someone a visit."

Eighteen - Lawyer Up

They'd tossed their firefighting overalls long before they reached the city. The upside to being in Danlí Prison was they didn't provide bright orange prison garbs, which meant they could blend in. Jack's T-shirt was soaked in sweat and he kept pulling at it as they arrived in the city and did their best to stay out of sight. With evening upon them, and darkness shrouding their movements, he figured that the guards wouldn't be looking in the city. They would expect them to make a run for the border.

"You think he can help?"

"No, but without money we aren't getting out of here and this bastard owes me."

They darted across the street heading for the cigar store. It was still open. A light glimmered from inside. They slipped down the back alley and made their way around to the back. Jack vaulted up onto the wall and was getting over when three dogs came rushing out of nowhere. Taken aback by the sudden assault, he nearly lost his balance. They were the same dogs from José's home. Two of them were jumping up trying to get at his leg. Jack climbed back over and hopped down.

Someone shouting in Spanish tried to calm the dogs but they weren't paying any attention.

"Well that won't work," Noah said.

"Then in the front entrance it is."

Jack knew they would be armed. He remembered they had one security guard on the door the day he visited. At the corner of the alley, Jack peered around and looked up and down the street before moving out. They hugged the wall tight until they reached the entrance. From the moment he stepped inside, the guard looked at him.

"We're closing in ten minutes."

"José in?" Jack asked.

He gave a nod and they walked on into the store section of the factory.

"I'll go get him," the security guard muttered in Spanish. Jack knew the second he saw him, the shit would hit the fan. He watched as the security guard buzzed himself in through a door using a card. Jack motioned to Noah and he rushed over and stuck his foot in before it closed. Not wasting any time, they ventured into the corridor beyond the door and watched the security guard stroll down to an office. He stopped and thumbed over his shoulder. Meanwhile Noah and Jack positioned themselves across the hall waiting for them to return. He could hear José asking who it was but the security guard had forgot to ask. José reprimanded him and said he could be replaced.

Jack prepared as the sound of their boots echoed in the corridor. The security guard was the first one that came into his line of sight. He'd already told Noah to grab his gun while he disabled him. Jack lunged forward and grabbed him around the neck while Noah grasped the gun and pulled it from its holster.

Like a rat about to be pounced on by a cat, José fled towards his office, almost slipping while Noah held a gun on the guard. Jack raced after him. Just as José was about to slam the door on him, Jack barged in knocking him back.

"How did you get out?"

"It's good to see you too, José. Take a seat."

Jack grabbed him up by the collar and dumped his ass on a chair.

"You shouldn't be here. No, you need to go."

Jack grabbed a chair and turned it around and plunked himself down. "I'm not going anywhere until you hand over the fifty thousand."

José scowled. "What are you on about?"

Jack breathed in, smiled and then lunged forward and plowed his fist into his face.

"Don't fuck with me. How much did you pay them?"

Holding his bloody nose and groaning like a bitch he shook his head. "I don't know what you are on about."

"Wrong answer."

Jack grabbed a hold of him and threw him across his desk, sending paperwork and a cup of coffee all over the floor.

"It wasn't me. It was Lázaro. He told me to set it up."

"And Noah?"

"That was nothing to do with either of us. That was his own stupidity."

Jack grabbed a hold of him and pushed him back into his chair. "I swear, it was Lázaro."

"So you must have got a cut from it."

"Twenty thousand. He has the rest."

"Where is it?"

José was reluctant to say. Jack grabbed the back of his head and slammed it against the table.

"In my safe. I'll get it for you."

Jack wiped his hands on the back of José's shirt. All the while, Noah stood in the doorway by the guard who was now on the floor.

"Guessing you have done this before?" Noah said. Jack didn't reply. He wanted that money and then they were getting the hell out of there. Twenty thousand was more than enough, but he would still pay Lázaro a visit before they returned to the USA. No one fucked him over.

The sniffling little asshole got down on his hands and knees and turned over the safe's dial until it unlocked. When it popped open, Jack leaned in and grabbed out what money he had inside. There was over twenty thousand but he wouldn't take any more than he was owed. He thumbed through it until he had his cut then he turned back to the table, grabbed a phone and slammed it down in front of José.

"Call Lázaro. Tell him you have just had a phone call from me and that I'm waiting at the airport."

He shook his head. "No. I'm not going to do that. He'll kill me."

"I'll kill you if you don't. Ten seconds."

Jack counted down. He'd about reached the end of his rope. José stared at the phone, then glanced at the guard.

"Time's a ticking, José."

José leaned forward and placed the call. He held several tissues to his face to catch the steady trickle of blood seeping from his nose. He had one hell of a welt on his forehead. Jack listened as the call went to voicemail.

José shrugged.

"Try his cell."

José tried again. This time he got through. All the time he was on the call, Jack kept a firm grip on the back of his neck. Occasionally he would squeeze it just to let him know what was going to happen if he tried to screw them over.

Once he hung up, Jack smiled and patted him on the back of the head like a dog.

"Right, get over there," Noah said to the security guard. They tied and gagged both of them and shoved them inside a closet. Once it was closed, Noah looked at Jack and smiled.

"Mother never told me about what you did for a living. I have a feeling I know why now."

Nineteen - Warden

The vehicle purred as he pulled out of the Honduran-Cuban Tobacco Company. He'd snatched up the keys to José's vehicle and planned on using it until they could dump it and pay for another. They were hours away from getting out of Honduras.

"I don't see why we have to risk heading to his place."

"No, you wouldn't."

"What's that supposed to mean?" Noah asked.

Sirens could be heard in the distance. Hopefully they were making their way towards the airport. Lázaro probably had gone with them but he wasn't taking any chances. Jack had taken a Cold Python gun belonging to José and Noah had the security guard's weapon.

"Do you ever tell her the truth?"

"Of course, but you don't know her, Jack, like I do. She would fly off the handle if she knew what I was involved in. She thinks I'm helping out with a missionary organization."

"The longer you keep her in the dark, the more pissed off she will be when she finds out."

The car wound its way through the valley towards the home of Lázaro. The lights of cars streaked past, blinding his vision.

"She won't find out."

"No?"

Noah stared at him. "Anyway, so what's the deal with you?"

"She never mentioned me?" Jack asked.

"Not until recently."

"Do you know you had a sister?"

"What happened to her?"

"Murdered by the Mafia," Jack muttered.

"So that's what you did before this?"

He nodded. "Been out of it for a while now."

"Trying to turn over a new leaf, huh?"

"Something like that."

As they got closer to Lázaro's property, Jack swerved

the vehicle off to the side and killed the engine. "We'll walk from here."

He planned on entering the place from the beach side but then opted to cut through the neighbor's property. Floodlights came on as they raced across a stranger's yard. They hauled themselves over a fence until they were around the side of the home. Jack figured he'd have surveillance cameras, maybe even a security guard or two. They hugged the side of the home as they made their way around to the back. Jack peered in through a window and saw Lázaro inside.

"Fuck."

He assumed he would be gone but instead he was sitting in front of a fireplace sipping on wine.

"You still want to do this?" Noah asked.

Jack checked how many rounds were inside the magazine before slamming it back inside.

"Wait here."

"Why?"

"Because I said so. If this goes south, I want you to

take the money and get out. Purchase a vehicle, get over the border. Do whatever you need to."

"I'm not leaving you here."

"I didn't come all this way and go through hell to have you dick me around," Jack said while eyeing Lázaro inside. The lights were dim. Just a few side lights offered illumination. If he was there, security couldn't be far. He glanced up looking for where the cameras were but there were none visible. He shuffled along the ground and reached up and tried the sliding door. It slipped open. He glanced back at Noah and nodded, then ventured inside. Wood crackled in the fire, and classical piano music played softly in the background. To think this asshole was living in the lap of luxury, all paid for by his own criminal behavior, pissed Jack off to no end.

He moved quietly up behind Lázaro and placed the gun to the back of his head and cocked it. As it clicked over, Lázaro didn't put his hands up or even act scared, he continued to sip his wine.

"Remember what I said about the fifty thousand. I

told you I would keep hold of it in case you tried to waste my time. And once again you are wasting my time," Lázaro muttered without turning.

"Where is it?"

"Oh, you won't be needing it."

Shadows flickered on the wall and Jack turned to see four armed guards come into the room holding submachine guns.

"Who's to say I won't shoot you right here?" Jack said. "Hell, I've got nothing to lose."

"For the same reason you didn't kill José." Lázaro rose from his chair while Jack kept his finger against the trigger. "And believe me, you should have killed him. I was minutes from home, heading to the airport when I got the call from José." He turned to face Jack. "One of his employees heard him yelling and let him out."

Jack shrugged. "It changes nothing. Where is the money?"

"Really? You still think you have a chance? The moment you pull that trigger, they'll kill you."

"Maybe so, but at least I'll know I took you with me."

Lázaro cast a glance over to his men and they parted and another man pushed forward Noah. He fell down on his knees.

"Are you sure about that?"

Jack looked at Noah and sighed. Lázaro reached and took the gun from Jack.

"Take them back, and throw them in the hole."

Jack gritted his teeth as they were strong-armed out of the home, loaded into the back of a truck and taken back to Danlí Prison.

* * *

This was why he worked alone. It was another reason why he was hesitant to help his mother. If anything went wrong, he couldn't keep an eye on Noah and his mother. As the steel door slammed behind him and he gazed around at the stone cell, he heard Noah's voice.

"Jack."

He didn't respond. He was in no mood for a conversation, especially with someone who had lied to his mother and had essentially screwed them both over. Jack ambled over to the steel-framed bed without a mattress and laid down on it. He stared up into the small gap and watched the stars.

Why hadn't Lázaro killed them? It would have been easier to have shot them in the house and claimed it was a home invasion. None of the police would have batted an eye. Hell, he could have even sold their organs on the black market. What advantage was there to keeping them locked up?

In the Mafia there were two rules of thought. One was to kill, the other was to punish. His old boss Gafino enjoyed torturing his victims, other mob bosses would just set people up and get them locked away. Inside, behind bars, they could inflict an endless amount of pain on them. It was the ultimate torture. Then, when they had grown tired of them, they could just pay to have someone kill them.

Perhaps that was it.

"Was he right?" Noah hollered.

Jack was laid back on the bed with his hands behind his head gazing up at the sky.

"About?"

"The reason you didn't kill José."

Jack pondered the question again. He had no qualms about putting a bullet in someone's head, if it was justified. He left the mob for a reason. He was tired of the killing. Any idiot could kill, it took strength to walk away. Isabel had taught him that. There would always be those freaks out there who got off on the blood, but Jack wasn't one of them. It had nothing to do with going soft. It would take a lifetime for him to change and he had all but used up his best years. No, it was about being tactical. It was about having a choice. He turned away from the mob. He chose to walk away from that lifestyle. He chose to help those who couldn't help themselves. And he would continue to choose who would live or die.

They remained in the hole for the better part of four days. Jack used the time doing sit-ups, push-ups, pull-ups, anything to keep the blood pumping and his mind clear.

Noah continued to pepper him with questions about his past. The past was just that, something behind him. A vague memory. He didn't want to remember it or let it shape his future. And he didn't want his younger brother thinking it was anything more than a brutal life. Instead he told him about Eddie Carmine. His father.

If there was anything good he could pass on to him, it would be what he'd learned from Eddie.

"So that's how he earned his living?"

"That's it," Jack replied.

"And you? You followed in his footsteps?"

"It's better than what I did before."

There was silence between them.

"Will you teach me? I mean if we get out of here."

Jack snorted. Before he could reply, the sound of guards making their way down to his cell echoed off the walls. A key clanked inside the keyhole and then the door opened. It was a guard and Chepe.

"Let's go."

"Where?"

"To fight."

Twenty - Cage Fight

The sky was a deep blue, without a cloud in sight as Jack emerged into the courtyard. When his eyes adjusted to the light, he shuffled along through a crowd of testosterone-fueled men waiting to see a good fight. As he rounded a corner into where men would play soccer, he saw a steel cage. It had to have been at least thirty feet across and seven feet high, made from iron bars, chain-link fencing and chicken wire. Beyond the wall, high in the corner tower was Lázaro and several businessmen. José was also among them, though looking a little weathered. A white adhesive bandage covered his nose. In their hands were bottles of beer, and they were smoking cigars.

Jack was thrust inside the cage and the iron gate closed behind him. Men on the outside jeered as another inmate elbowed his way through the crowd. All of them had received the same pitch: that if they won, one year would be dropped off their sentence. So like anyone staring down twenty or more years, they were more than eager to enter.

His opponent's name was Alejandro. He was twice the size of Jack but about the same in height. His beard was overgrown and he had tattoos all over his body. One coordinator pushed him forward and he retaliated by throwing him into the crowd. *Great,* Jack thought. *A lunatic.*

The gate opened, and Alejandro grinned as he stepped inside. He hopped up and down as if trying to pump himself up, he slapped his own face a few times and then circled the cage. Jack stared up at Lázaro and scowled.

There was no way out of this.

No bargaining.

The crowd went quiet as they waited for some signal from Lázaro. He dropped a white cloth over the edge and it drifted down like a snowflake. In the few seconds it took to fall, they could have heard a pin drop. The second it touched the courtyard, Alejandro charged forward. Jack spun around and back kicked him in the gut then followed through with a punch to the face. He hit the ground and groaned. Jack didn't wait for him to get up, he landed on top of his neck with his knee and fired his fist into his ribs until he heard the bones break.

Then he rose and looked back up at Lázaro. Chepe looked as if he was taking instructions from him on the ground through a radio. He hurried over to the cage and shouted to Jack.

"Finish him."

"Fuck you!" Jack said strolling over to the gate and demanding for them to open it. The crowd chanted in Spanish, over and over again, "Terminar."

Jack shook on the cage door but it wouldn't open. With all the noise of the crowd he didn't see Alejandro get up again. He felt his fist slam into the back of his kidney and then he was thrown across the cage. Lying on the floor for a second, he watched as the man staggered over to him and raised his leg. Jack rolled as it came down, and again as he tried to stamp on him. Rearing back his leg, Jack thrust it up into his groin making him double over in pain. The inmates were going wild. Lázaro and the other businessmen were laughing. Jack got up and followed through with a knee to the man's face causing him to collapse.

"Enough!" Jack shouted. But it wasn't over. Alejandro wouldn't let broken ribs or a few bruises keep him from an early release. Desperation blocked out pain and when he stepped into that cage he was prepared to die if need be. One way or another he was getting out of that prison. Jack shook his head.

Alejandro stumbled to his feet gripping his side, blood trickling out the corner of his mouth. He waved Jack forward.

"Come on."

"You want out?" Jack replied. He rushed towards him and did a flying kick into his chest sending him hurtling back against the cage. Jack raced over, grabbed him around the neck and fell backwards on the ground while pulling hard to the left.

His neck cracked as Jack wrenched on it. Alejandro's

body went limp.

In his lifetime, Jack had killed people for many reasons. Some might justify what he had just done as self-defense. That didn't sit well. He slipped out from beneath him and the cage door was opened. Jack glanced up at Lázaro and watched him exchanging money with the businessmen. The inmates meant nothing to him. It was all about the green.

As soon as he stepped out, he was taken over to meet with Lázaro, who stood on one side of the iron bars and clapped his hands.

"Now that is what I'm talking about. See, I had a good feeling about you."

"Fuck you."

"Oh, come now, Jack. You just bought yourself a year off your sentence. Only eighteen more fights to go and you're a free man."

Jack leaned in close to the cage and eyed him and José. "When I get out of here, I'm coming for you."

He snorted. "I love your confidence."

Lázaro turned to leave and Jack spat a big wad of phlegm over the back of his white jacket. Lázaro twisted around, his eyes flared.

"And I was going to let you stay in general population. Take him back to the hole."

Crowds of inmates cheered as they led him away. Inside the walls, respect was earned by one's ability to survive.

"Jack? Is that you?" Noah called out as they passed by his cell before he was led into his own. The door slammed behind him.

Jack stared down at his bloodied knuckles, his hands trembling with adrenaline still pumping through him. Was it him? Oh yeah, it was him. Blood. Death. Violence. He wasn't losing himself in here, he was finding himself again.

Twenty One - Plans

Fights didn't occur every day, at least not the ones that were arranged by the warden. Those occurred once a week. That meant four people were dying every month. Who was keeping tabs on deaths? The prison system was nothing like America. There would have been a public outcry, the prison board would have wanted answers and the media would have been all over it but not down here. The entire place was a human rights violation. The conditions were inhuman, the food barely edible and what prison in the world allowed inmates to carry batons? Only here. It was clear to see why Lázaro lived in the lap of luxury. He had it made here. The government didn't care how prisoners were being treated. Death was a weekly event. And the death of a hardened criminal just meant one less mouth to feed. It was a win-win situation. Criminals were off the street, the inmates had an outlet for their rage, guards barely had to risk their lives and the warden was getting filthy rich off the sale of body parts.

No one spoke out as no one had a need.

Inmates assumed they would earn their freedom, and with only one fight arranged each week, there was an endless line of prisoners eager to be the next to step inside the cage.

Over the course of the next four weeks, Jack and Noah fought several inmates, each time they won but there was always the chance that the next time they entered it would be the last.

Jack was in his cell doing push-ups when he heard Noah return, he was coughing hard and groaning. This time it didn't sound like they walked him back, it almost sounded as if he was being dragged.

He paused and called out to him.

"Noah. You okay?"

A cell door slammed and he heard another groan. Jack asked again.

"I'm still alive if that's what you're asking," he croaked out a reply before spitting.

A few more days passed before they released them back into the general population. The warden had brought in Jack to say how pleased he was with the way things were going. He said his cooperation hadn't gone unnoticed.

It was all lip service. Bullshit, just to keep them fighting.

Every day inside that hole he was thinking of how to get out. Jack's head jerked as he was shoved into the courtyard. A guard locked the door behind him and he went about searching for Noah. He found him smoking a cigarette at the far end of the courtyard. He was chatting with an inmate known as Carlos. He was part of a violent gang called Barrio 18, otherwise known as M18 or the 18th Street Gang. Though they were recognized for their bald heads, and tattoos, it was for their murders that most Hondurans knew them. Originating in Los Angeles, Barrio 18 and the gang called Mara Salvatrucha had pretty much carved up Honduras. They weren't gangs to be fucked with and they earned their respect on the streets through pure violence and dismembering their victims.

Danlí was full of members of both. It was one of the first things Ernesto warned him about.

"Don't get in the middle of them. Don't pick a side. Don't even look at them."

And here was Noah having a full-blown conversation.

"What's going on?" Jack said pulling Noah to one side as Carlos returned to his fellow gang members. Across the yard the Mara Salvatrucha crew looked on through narrowed eyes.

"Pueblo killed Henry last night."

Jack sighed. It was only a matter of time. After the incident on the mountain, Henry had been placed in medical to treat his wounds, though once healed up he was sent back to general population without any protection.

"He visited his cell, and after raping him, Pueblo stabbed him to death."

"And the guards just watched?"

"Watched? They don't watch, they turn a blind eye. It's all about who you know and how much you have in here, Jack."

"And M18?"

"That's why I'm speaking to them. We can't keep going like this. We need people to unite. It's the only way out of here, Jack. The last time they had a riot, they gained control of the prison and from there they were able to negotiate with the warden. That's why the coordinators run this place. Now I'm thinking if we all refuse to fight, what are they going to do?"

"Good luck with that. There are too many in here who believe it's their ticket out."

"Maybe. But what if we could prove that wasn't the case?"

"What do you have in mind?"

Noah scanned the yard and took a puff on his cigarette before handing it to Jack.

"We're not the only ones who know what the warden is doing. Chepe knows. Rumor has it that he meets with the warden on a weekly basis to discuss prison matters. What if we could get him to work with us? Carlos knows him well."

Jack shook his head. "Chepe has it made here. He's the head honcho. You think he will risk what he has for us, or any of the inmates in here? You are out of your mind."

"Then we revolt. Get both gangs to start a riot. There are only twelve guards on shift, Jack."

"Yeah, I'm pretty sure the others aren't far away."

"Who cares!"

"Just leave it."

Jack went to walk away.

"Leave it? What, and die in the cage? It's only a matter of time."

"You should have thought about that when you tried to sneak drugs out of this country."

Noah rushed over and spun Jack around. "You act as though your slate is clean but it's far from perfect."

"No, you're right. But this isn't the way. Gangs don't unite and they won't riot again."

"How can you be sure?"

"Because they know the warden has them by the balls.

One mistake in here and they will lose what little privileges they have. That includes family visits."

Wednesdays, Saturdays and Sundays, inmates could have family visit the prison, some of the wives even stayed overnight in the cells. Ernesto said it was just another means of keeping the inmates from losing their cool.

"But if they get out of here, they can be with their families all the time."

Jack turned back to Noah. He wasn't seeing the bigger picture. "Wake up, Noah. Look around you. What do you see?"

He gazed around. Men lingered close to the walls, some did menial tasks, others played soccer, while the rest smoked, lifted weights and ran their own little stores where they sold bottles of soda, packets of chips and barely edible food out of fridges.

"I see desperation."

"No. You see people not complaining. Beyond these walls are slums. Hell, most of the people in here have it better off than those out there. At least here they get three square meals a day. It might taste like shit but they didn't have to pay for it. Now if they have money they can make their life inside here a little easier but don't think for one minute that everyone in here wants to get out."

"Of course they do."

"Really? Then why is it that while some of these people in here can get early release if they go through the rehabilitation and read books, that most of them don't do it?"

He shrugged. "Maybe they forget. Maybe they don't believe it will happen."

"Or maybe, they prefer it inside," Jack added.

Noah shifted his weight to his back foot and poked his finger into his own chest. "You think I'm out of my mind." He scoffed. "You want to stay in here, fine. But I'm off to look for an alternative."

Jack grabbed him by the arm but he shrugged him off.

With that said, Noah trudged off. Jack hadn't given up on escaping but they had to play this smart. They were in a country that was driven by poverty and greed. The only way they would make it across the border, if and when they escaped, was with money.

Across the yard, he saw several members of both gangs looking his way. Gangs were only loyal to their kind. Noah was playing with fire. If for any reason the Mara Salvatrucha thought he was trying to stir up trouble between them and the 18th Street Gang members, he was liable to get his throat slit.

Twenty Two - Harvesting

It was huge business. He couldn't believe he hadn't thought of it sooner. Lázaro looked over his bank account and sipped on an ice-cold beer while relishing the fact that in a few years he could retire. He had no intentions of remaining the warden for Danlí. Sure, it was profitable but greed was a stumbling block, and one he didn't plan on tripping over.

He looked over the updated price list he'd received from José's contact that morning.

Corneas — $30,000

Lungs — $150,000

Heart — $130,000

Liver — $98,000

Stomach — $508

Scalp — $627

Coronary artery — $1,525

Skull and teeth — $1,200

Pint of blood — $337

Hand and forearm — $385

Gallbladder — $1,219

Kidney — $262,000

Small intestine — $2,519

Skin — $10 per square inch

At first, he'd balked at the idea when José presented it to him a few years back. If he hadn't been a close friend and confidant of his, he would have called the cops on him. But after crunching the numbers it was hard to not be intrigued. Once José laid out how it could be done and they could get away with it, he entertained the thought. Of course he didn't just agree and rush into it. No, they had to be careful. There were several things to consider. Some families would want to bury their loved ones. Then there was the paperwork involved. Every death had to be accounted for. Sure, the system was corrupt and most in government didn't give two shits about a criminal's life, but it only took one mistake and the powers that be would come down on him, if only to protect their own asses.

For the operation to run smoothly, it would require several people to be involved. José would cover the legal side of things and ensure that all paper trails were covered. He then used a doctor who was already involved in the black market. Someone who could easily be manipulated and deal with the removal of parts.

Next, it was just a matter of deciding on who and when.

Initially organs were harvested from the dead bodies of inmates who had died in fights or had been killed by another inmate. At first, he wasn't greedy. He took internal parts that wouldn't be seen by loved ones. Heart, liver, kidneys, and some of the expensive organs. If the man had no family, they took it all.

Once he saw the money roll in, it was too good to pass up. That's when he looked at how they could increase the number of deaths in the prison while making sure that those inside wouldn't open their mouths.

That's when the idea of early release came to him.

There was no way in hell he would let those maggots out early but they didn't know that. All he had to do was sell them on the hope. They were desperate for even a smidgen of light at the end of the tunnel.

Four fights a month, four deaths wouldn't raise too many eyebrows.

He had set up a system inside by using Chepe. He was already being paid a handsome amount of money each month, and a reduced sentence, to keep the inmates in order but when the idea of cage fighting was laid before him, he couldn't resist. A few hundred dollars to have his coordinators make folks believe they were getting released. A couple of early releases by those that fought to get the inmates to believe it was all legit.

The rest was like taking candy from a child.

And to top it off, he had two of his closest business friends swing by for the fights and lay bets down. It was good fun, and profitable business.

Lázaro leaned back in his chair and eyed José over the top of his drink.

"Good work, José. Anything you need to tell me? I notice you have been acting a little on edge."

"It's that American."

"Winchester?"

José nodded.

"Yeah, he's an interesting one. A wild card, though he's earning us a nice little nest egg."

"I don't like it, Lázaro. How many other inmates would have risked showing up at your home after escaping?"

"Does it matter?"

José leaned forward in his seat and brushed his hair back to show a gnarly scar on the top of his forehead. "Yes, it matters. I could have died."

Lázaro scoffed while glancing over the sheet again and doing a few numbers in his head. He was half listening to José and half thinking about how they might up the ante.

"Look, if you're worried about Winchester, don't be. I've been thinking about how we can increase the body count. You know, speed up the process. At the rate money is coming in from the organs we're harvesting, we could have more than enough to retire in one to two years from now. However, if someone was to cause a riot, that could speed up things."

"You've got to be joking?"

"Forty-two inmates died in the last one. That's a shitload of cash that would take us ten weeks to earn with the weekly cage fights."

"About that." José placed his bottle of beer on the table. "People are talking."

"What do you mean?"

"On the streets, people are talking about the fights. I don't know how it's got out but people know."

"Well, I guess it was only a matter of time."

"And that doesn't bother you?" José said.

Lázaro shook his head. "No, why should it? As far as anyone is concerned it's just another way for the inmates to blow off some steam."

"Blow off some steam? Openly killing others?"

"You had no problem with it when it was lining your

pockets. Are you having doubts about our little operation, José? Because if you are, I need to know now."

"I have no problem with the fights but this wasn't part of the plan. For close to a year we have been careful. It's the reason we haven't been caught. We did the fights and those who ended up in the infirmary were put out of their misery. But allowing an inmate to kill in front of another? You must have known that someone would start talking."

"I'll have Chepe look into it. You worry too much, and you give Winchester way too much credit."

Lázaro snorted. Maybe they had become a little lax but he'd been curious to test the waters. See how far he could push the inmates and keep them under his control. Some would have called it a power trip, an egotistical need to dominate those below him but it wasn't anything to do with that. It was all about incentive. Inmates could fight any time they liked. In a way, it was a double incentive. The inmates thought they would get their freedom, whether it was from winning enough fights or exiting the prison in a body bag when they lost.

It was freedom.

And a hell of a lot better than staring down a life sentence.

Anyway, he hadn't made it this far without having a few public officials and police officers on payroll. That was the beauty of a corrupt government. Everyone had a price to remain silent.

Twenty Three - Bloodthirsty

Jack heard the chanting long before he saw Pueblo. His hands were bound in white tape, his shirt off, exposing every scar. Chepe led him between the line of inmates repeating Pueblo's name. He figured it was only a matter of time before he faced him. Pueblo paced back and forth inside the cage, glaring as Jack got close to the gate. As always, he looked up towards the tower where Lázaro stood with excited anticipation spread across his face. The gate groaned and he stepped inside and heard it seal behind him.

"I'm gonna fuck you up," Pueblo said.

Jack leaned his head from side to side to loosen up. Both of them watched as the cloth settled. Pueblo charged forward throwing his entire weight into Jack's stomach like an American football tackle. Jack rained elbow blows down on his back even as he was forced back against the cage. Pueblo pounded his ribs and kidneys with jab after jab until Jack kneed him in the gut and shoved him back.

In an instant, he surged forward unleashing multiple left jabs, and a right hook to the soft temple. That was always the key. Connect bone with soft spots. Pueblo stumbled back and shook his head. Jack swung again though this time he ducked and parried with an uppercut that rattled him and wobbled his legs. Pueblo then did some kind of spinning kick knocking Jack off balance. He landed on the ground only to feel Pueblo grab him and throw his weight back, causing Jack to flip and land hard.

The crowd cheered and called for his death.

His senses were shaken as he rolled over and attempted to get up only to be kicked in the face and land flat on his back. Pueblo straddled him and squeezed his larynx. He was strong. The strength that came from spending every day pumping weights in the courtyard, for months on end. And yet that would be his downfall.

Size mattered little to Jack. Neither did the appearance of a ripped physique. With muscle came stiffness and that meant he moved slower. Jack reached around with both hands and forced his thumbs into his eye sockets causing him to scream in pain and back off.

Coughing hard and trying to regain his composure, Jack didn't hear the batons land inside the cage, though he moved just in time to see Pueblo scoop one up and come at him. He reared back his leg and fired it into his gut, making him land hard.

Now up on his feet, he staggered over to the second baton and grabbed it. A quick glance up at Lázaro to fuel his anger and Jack rushed back over to Pueblo and struck him as hard as he could across the back, face and legs. His wrist was grabbed and he parried it by swiping his legs out from beneath him and driving the baton hard into the center of his gut.

The back and forth went on for what seemed like ten minutes before both men were battered and gasping for air.

From across the cage, even Pueblo looked as if he was questioning continuing. There was reluctance in his eyes. He stared up at Lázaro, shook his head and trudged forward. A few feet from each other, a glimmer of silver shot into view. A single machete landed in the center of the cage. Their eyes widened as they looked at each other and then both raced for it.

Pueblo did another spinning kick and caught Jack just on the tip of the chin sending blood spewing from his mouth. He landed hard and his baton shot across the cage, and through a gap. He turned to see Pueblo pick up the machete and spin it a few times in his hand.

"Terminar!" the crowd chanted, thirsty for blood.

Dazed, and with pain coursing through him, Jack used all his strength to rise to his feet. Without a weapon, he had to judge distance, move fast and disarm him. Pueblo flashed a bloody grin and then shot forward swiping the air in front of him. His eyes were wild. Jack bounced back, ducked, shot to the right and spun a sidekick to his ribs. His heart was pounding against his chest as he slid to the left and grabbed his wrist. It wasn't the first time he'd been attacked with a blade. Hell, he'd spent his entire youth avoiding close calls. A few times he'd been cut, none had been deep enough to cause serious injury.

In that moment, he got tunnel vision. All he could see was Pueblo. He twisted and turned, forcing his arm upwards, then he pulled and struck with multiple knee shots to the solar plexus.

But Pueblo hadn't earned his place in the prison by being an easy kill. He swiped Jack's leg and allowed his entire body weight to fall against him. Both of them landed hard on the ground. Pueblo was on top trying now to decapitate Jack by forcing the machete downward. Jack had a hand on the handle and the other gripping the machete blade. It was cutting into his hand but he knew if he let go it would slice right through his throat.

Jack roared. It was like trying to bench press Pueblo's entire weight. The crazed look in his eyes made it clear that the fight wouldn't end without death.

There was no mercy in the cage.

Instead of trying to hold him back, he allowed Pueblo to get closer. Close enough that his one hand was near to Jack's mouth. That's when Jack clamped onto it with his teeth. His cry reverberated and overwhelmed the noise of the crowd. Jack bit through his finger causing him to release the blade and fall back in agony.

Breathing hard, he rolled to one side and spat a piece of his finger to the floor. With his one good hand, he rose and gazed down at Pueblo who was holding his hand as blood squirted out from his finger.

He glanced up, grimacing through the pain. Jack scooped up the machete.

"This is for Henry."

In one smooth motion, he brought that blade down into the back of Pueblo's neck. It sunk in like a knife through hot butter and Pueblo slumped forward. Still holding the blade, covered in blood, sweat and panting hard, Jack looked up.

A pin dropping to the concrete could have been heard.

The silence was broken by Lázaro clapping.

As the shock of Pueblo's death dissipated, the prisoners roared and chanted Jack's name. Among the crowd, he saw his brother Noah. He was nodding.

Will you teach me? He could hear Noah's words ringing in his ears.

This wasn't what he wanted to teach him.

Jack backed away from the machete, his hands dripping in blood.

Twenty Four - Refusal

The gate didn't open. Jack was still on his knees when he realized they weren't doing anything. He got up and crossed the dirt floor and shook the bars. The frail Honduran man who unlocked it stepped back and cast his gaze at the ground.

"Open up."

Jack looked around and saw Lázaro speaking into a radio. Chepe nodded and double-timed it over to a man from the M18 gang and then over to a group from the Mara Salvatrucha. They both looked confused. A quick prod with Chepe's baton and they were forced towards the cage. When Chepe reached the gate, Jack demanded to know what was going on.

"You fight again."

"What?"

The gate opened and Jack slammed his foot against it forcing it to hit Chepe in the face. A mistake he would no doubt pay for. After Chepe picked himself up off the ground, he touched his lip. It was cut and bleeding. He pointed his baton at Jack and cursed him before the two gang members entered the cage. They kept their distance from each other, looking unsure of what they should do. Any attempt by Jack to get out of the cage was met by force as several coordinators jabbed him hard in the face and gut.

Once the gate was closed, he turned to face Lázaro.

"No more. I'm done."

He pushed the blade through the cage, only to find Lázaro smirking. He shrugged as if to say, your loss. Then he dropped another white handkerchief. When it hit the ground, however, the two gang members didn't charge Jack. They stared at each other as if waiting to see if the other would react. Instead they turned and shook their heads.

Jack wasn't sure if they were protesting fighting altogether or whether it was just him.

Fury spread across Lázaro's face; he got on the radio

and once again Chepe looked flustered. He shouted something in Spanish at the men and then slammed his baton across the bars. They shook their heads and took a seat on the ground.

Had Noah got through to them?

It was impossible.

Two rival gangs with bad blood for one another. They would have jumped at the chance to kill each other. But it wasn't each other they were being instructed to kill, it was Jack.

Fear wasn't an issue. These gang members lived in the realm of fear. They thrived on it.

Carlos on the outside of the cage stood among the rest of his people shaking his head.

More shouting ensued and then the gate opened. Jack was dragged out by several of the coordinators along with the two gang members. Lázaro and the others in the tower disappeared out of sight and Jack assumed he would be taken down to the hole and left to rot in there for another few weeks. But Lázaro had something far worse in store.

Once the crowds were dispersed, Jack and the two gang members were led over to a wall where their hands were shackled. The chains were then slipped through iron rings and they were hoisted until their toes barely touched the ground. There was a gang member either side of him.

Five minutes later Lázaro emerged inside the compound escorted on either side by armed guards who kept the prisoners at bay. He made his way over. Wearing a light brown suit, shades and a hat, he smiled as he got closer. He didn't bother to speak to the gang members, instead he targeted Jack.

He flipped up the visor on his sunglasses and looked Jack up and down.

"You are only making things worse for you."

"Maybe, but at least I get the satisfaction you won't get what you want. I'm done fighting."

"I'll decide that."

Jack could feel his muscles tighten. He wanted to lash out at him but they had bound his ankles.

Lázaro then turned his attention to the two gang members. "How long do you think it will be before these two will break? Before they will fight in the cage?"

The two members cursed and spat at Lázaro. He reacted by making Chepe strike both of them in the stomach with his baton. It was noon. Under the heat of the blistering sun it wouldn't take long before they would break.

"Doesn't matter. I'm done fighting."

"Then you will be an easy kill."

"Don't you mean an easy sell?" Jack replied.

Lázaro turned his attention to Jack. "I aim to please those who bid."

"On the fight or our organs?"

Lázaro narrowed his gaze, he took the baton from Chepe and dug it hard into Jack's stomach, putting his full weight on it. Jack heaved trying to get air.

"It's hard, isn't it? You know it takes very little strength to stop a man's breathing if you know where to apply pressure."

245

"I'll remember that when I strangle you," Jack said.

He let out a laugh, turned to Chepe for a moment and then struck Jack across the knees. Jack groaned but gritted his teeth. He wouldn't give this asshole the satisfaction of breaking him down.

"You should have fled when you had the chance."

"Where would the fun be in that?" Jack replied.

Lázaro handed the baton back to Chepe. "No food or water for the rest of the day. They'll soon come around."

With that said he walked away leaving them to hang there in the blistering heat. The rest of the inmates weren't allowed to come near them, nor use the courtyard. They were doing it to set an example. To make it painfully obvious that refusal was not an option.

One hour stretched into two, then three and Jack lost track of how long they had been hanging there. His lips were dry and throat parched. With their heads hung low, each of them dealt with it in his own way. The gang member on his right cursed Jack, while the other told him to shut the hell up.

"Why didn't you fight?" Jack asked the one on his left.

He was hesitant to reply but then he spoke. "I can't speak for him but my brother died in the cage."

Twenty Five - Resistance

That evening it rained harder than it ever had. The dirt below Jack's feet turned into a mini-stream, washing away the grime of the day. Mixed into the steady flow was the blood of Pueblo. Every few hours Chepe would come by and ask if they were ready to fight. Neither of them said yes. Jack wasn't sure why the man on his right hadn't fought. He had been nothing but belligerent to him since they chained them up. He went by the name Darrel. The one on the left who had spoken with him was called Esau. He came to learn that Esau's brother was one of the first to fight. At the start, there was no mention of an early release. Fights were put on for the pleasure of Lázaro. Selection of fighters was random. Esau's brother's name was called out and though he was ill, he was forced to fight. Esau pleaded for them to let him take his place but Lázaro wouldn't let him.

Jack turned his head. Darrel had barely spoken a word

in hours. He'd been pretty sure he would be the first one to break and agree to fight but he hadn't.

"Darrel, why didn't you fight?"

Though he didn't reply, he shot Jack a sideways glance. His hard exterior was fading as the strain of being strung up and made to bake in the sun and shiver in the rain had worn him down.

"How long have you been a gang member?" Jack asked.

"Since I was a kid."

"You've always been with M18?"

He nodded. It was common to see gang members drawing young kids in at an age when they were impressionable. Most came from broken homes or abusive families, or they grew up as orphans. There were those who fell in with the wrong crowd but they rarely lasted. It didn't matter where he went, gangs were the same. No different than the Mafia. It gave people a sense of belonging, it made them feel valued and more than anything it gave them hope in the face of a bleak future.

Esau made a remark about M18's being pussies.

"Fuck you, homie," Darrel spat back.

Jack chuckled.

"What's funny?"

"This. Gangs. Life. It's all the same, just wrapped up in more bullshit."

"What the fuck would you know about being in a gang?"

"Because I worked for the mob, asshole."

"Who you calling asshole?"

"Listen, you want to keep playing this game of jerking each other off over the next ten years, then knock yourself out. But if you want to get out of here, you're gonna have to lay aside your differences and work together."

"No fucking chance," Esau said.

"Like he said," Darrel replied.

"Right, because your homies wouldn't like it. It goes against all you are," Jack said in a mocking manner. Both of them grumbled.

"There is nothing that can be done," Esau said.

"Not if you work alone. But together."

"Simón wouldn't go for it."

"Who's that?"

"Mara Salvatrucha leader," Darrel replied before Esau could answer. "Guy doesn't have the balls to do anything."

"And M18 does? You're full of shit," Esau said.

"Actually, Carlos is down with starting a riot. Hell, he's been thinking of kicking it off since the last one."

"Doubt it."

"Whatever, man. It's the reason I didn't fight."

"Because of Carlos?"

He nodded.

Jack remembered Carlos making a gesture from within the crowd.

The rest of the evening was spent in misery. Chilled to the bone and drenched until the sun came up.

* * *

Two days passed before all three of them were released from the shackles and sent to the infirmary to get cleaned up and checked over. Lázaro wasn't having a change of heart; he was just making a statement, sending a clear message to the rest of the prison about the consequences of defying his orders.

After being released, all three of them could barely stand. Hungry, thirsty and having not used their legs in over forty-eight hours, they were carried out. Had it not been for the rain, they would have been in an even worse state. The looks on the faces of the inmates brought home the reality of what might be done if they resisted.

From inside the infirmary Jack could hear the noise of the crowd as the warden returned to pitting them against each other. Lázaro had succeeded. Of course he would. Not everyone would have stood in defiance. As long as the house was divided, it would remain that way.

There was still something that puzzled Jack. A question that needed answering.

Once he had spent a few days in the infirmary and was led back to his cell, he sought out Carlos from the M18 gang. He was seated at a table playing cards when Jack strolled up. Several of Carlos's men approached him to prevent him from getting close. Jack put up his hands to make it clear that he had no beef with him.

"A moment of your time, that's all I want."

Carlos tossed his cards down and told the others not to look at them or they'd be in trouble. He got up and walked past Jack leading him over to a fence.

He extended his arms out. "Speak."

"Your man Darrel was ready to fight. He said you prevented it from happening. Why?"

Carlos kicked a few loose stones at his feet and glanced over to his friends. "I wanted to test the water."

Jack's brow knit together. A look of confusion.

"In here. We live and die by our actions. I wanted to see where the Mara Salvatrucha stood."

"And if Esau had attacked me?"

"So would have Darrel."

"But you know the only reason he didn't was because of his brother. It wasn't anything to do with me. Esau has his own issues with Lázaro."

"Don't you think I know? There isn't anything that gets by my eyes in here."

"So?" Jack asked. "Will you speak with the Mara Salvatrucha?"

He scoffed. "Of course not."

Jack shook his head confused.

"You think I will go up to them and ask them to fight alongside us?"

"But Noah?"

Carlos leaned in. "I heard what your brother said and I agree but don't think for one moment I would do this for him, or you. You mean nothing."

"Then do it for yourselves. How many of your brothers must die to line the warden's pockets? There is no early release. He's harvesting organs on the black market. There is no winning. You need to get that through to Simón."

Carlos stepped in close and grabbed Jack by the collar. He wasn't a large man and he didn't strike fear into Jack but he allowed him to feel as though he was the dominant one.

"Hombre, I don't need to do anything."

"And yet you want freedom."

There was a tense moment between them. His eyes scanned his face. Jack knew that with just a glance from Carlos, the others would have lynched him before a guard could have done anything. The largest number of inmates inside the compound were gang members, and many were M18.

"The only way you, or any of them are getting out is by working together. Look at what you accomplished in the last riot. Now, I heard the crowds this morning. That can't happen."

"And what do you suggest?"

"Unite."

Carlos pulled a cigarette and lit it, he placed a hand on the chain-link fence and cast his gaze outside. "Outside, beyond these walls, no M18 has ever worked alongside a Mara Salvatrucha." He blew out gray smoke and shook his head. "You are speaking of things that can't be."

"And yet you all abide by the rules of Chepe and the coordinators, why?"

He spat at the ground and took another puff on his cigarette. "It's how it works in here."

"Then maybe that's how this can work. Perhaps neither of you need to agree upon a truce. You only have to agree to abide by what Chepe demands."

Jack took a few steps back. It was right there all along. He cast a glance across the yard to where Chepe was. He had a Band-aid across his nose from where Jack had smashed the gate into his face. Could he convince him?

As he stood there chewing it over, he saw several families coming in for visitation. Chepe greeted what looked to be his wife and two children. Beneath his hard exterior was this ordinary man with a family. How long was his sentence? Had he made a deal with Lázaro for early release? Questions bombarded his mind even as Carlos returned to the others. Carlos made it clear that if Jack could convince Chepe to resist and riot or if he could get Simón on board, he would have the cooperation of the M18s.

Jack pressed his back against the fence as Noah made his way over. He tapped him on the chest. "So, how did it go? Is he in?"

"That depends. How easy do you think it would be to turn the general coordinator?"

Noah blew his cheeks out. "If anyone has it good in here, it's Chepe. I would say even on his worst day, he wouldn't go against the warden. Especially, if he has come to some arrangement with the warden for an early release."

"Have you spoken with Simón?"

Noah nodded. "He won't do it."

"Fuck!" Jack said. He knew how pigheaded gang members could be. It was all about honor, appearances and respect. Just because they were locked up alongside their rivals, it didn't mean they would fight alongside them, even if it meant getting out.

"Look, Jack, I've been thinking. We need to just make a break for it. The next time they have us out on work duty."

"Noah, there won't be a next time. Lázaro won't risk it again." Jack breathed in deeply. His muscles still ached. "Besides, even if we could get out of here, you want this sick bastard to keep on doing this?"

"Who cares what he does? These are criminals in here. You look at them as if they're innocent. As if they deserve anything more than death. And anyway, do you really want to see these animals on the street?"

Jack turned to him. "Criminals or not, what Lázaro is doing is wrong."

"Of course. Listen, Jack, I applaud what you have done for others, but that was then, this is now. We've got to think about ourselves." He paused. "You were right, trying to bridge the gap between two rival gangs was absurd, and thinking Chepe could be turned, well…" He stopped talking.

"Maybe that's it. We're going about this the wrong way," Jack said.

"What?"

"We've been trying to go against the flow and get them to unite and riot against the warden. But he's out there. Chepe's in here. Without him, this place will fall like a house of cards."

Jack walked away.

"Where you going?" Noah asked.

"Off to start a riot."

He continued and then stopped and turned back to Noah.

"Well come on. You said you wanted to learn."

Noah smirked and followed Jack's lead.

Twenty Six - Blood Bath

Family day was the only time that Chepe was left by himself. It was the only time inmates' eyes were distracted. It was the only time wives were allowed in the cells. There was no privacy, well not like the U.S. conjugal visits. In the States, prisoners were assigned to designated rooms like a trailer or a cabin. They were even given things like condoms, lubricant, soap, bed linen and towels.

Not in Danlí.

It all took place in the same cell they shared with twenty other people. It was the reason they had drapes that hung over their bunk beds. No one in the prison system gave a shit. It was down to the inmate to secure privacy.

Over the time they had been there, Jack had observed the flow of the prison. Coordinators weren't any different. The only time they laid down those batons and gave

Chepe space was when his old lady showed up.

Today wasn't any different.

Jack knew there would be consequences to his actions. Kicking a gate in the face of the general coordinator might have got him a beat-down in a USA prison. But here? In front of an audience of inmates, it was all about getting respect back and Chepe would get it regardless of what plans the warden had for Jack.

Death was coming, and Jack wouldn't wait.

In the maze of shanty buildings, Jack watched as Chepe disappeared inside his cell with his wife and closed the barred door behind him. A drape was dropped and his kids played outside with a coordinator. They were rarely far from him unless he had that visit. Jack lit a cigarette and stood by the corner waiting for his visit to end.

All the while he looked at the kids. They couldn't have been over six or seven years old. By the time Chepe was released from prison they would be in their early twenties. He went back and forth in his mind on whether to kill him. He'd planned to take one of the M18's shirts, cover it in Chepe's blood and leave it inside a cell belonging to a member of the Mara Salvatrucha.

All hell would break loose once Chepe's body was found.

Accusations would fly and cells would be searched.

He was about to kill two birds with one stone.

If everything went to plan, in less than thirty minutes the shit would hit the fan.

While waiting, he watched families come and go. There was a different atmosphere when wives and kids came into the prison. Some inmates sat holding hands with their wives. The same individuals he'd seen acting all tough, and threatening. Others tossed their kids up in the air and hugged them. He'd always imagined that it would have been a hellish experience to bring kids into, but there was an unwritten rule. No one could touch another inmate's family. Fortunately, those who might have been inclined to break that rule were housed in a separate block, called cell 27. An isolated area designated only for those who had committed rape; pedophiles and violent sex offenders.

Jack heard the groan of a gate opening. He peered around the corner acting casual and like the previous two visits before, Chepe gave his wife a kiss, hugged his kids and the coordinator led them back to the exit. Chepe pulled out a tin of cigars and lit one, he turned and Jack looked away. When he glanced back he saw him disappear inside the cell.

He knew he had a window of only five minutes before the coordinator would return. Gripping the shirt that Noah had grabbed from the cell of one of the M18 members, he sprinted over and pulled out a shank that was made from a plastic toothbrush that had been filed down on a stone wall.

As he entered the cell, his eyes darted around the small corridor. Either side of him were wooden bunk beds, multicolored material was draped over the sides. He knew the beds were empty. Chepe was the only one that got real privacy. It was another perk of being a general coordinator.

He moved quietly. Inside he could smell cigar and hear Chepe shuffling around. As he rounded the corner to where his bunk was, he saw a light on behind the drape and what looked like the silhouette of Chepe.

Jack shot forward and ripped back the curtain only to find the covers had been stuffed with pillows.

There was a roar as Chepe burst out of a side bed and slammed into him, knocking the shank out of his hand.

There wasn't much that anyone could get by him.

Right here in the middle of the cramped quarters, Jack wrestled for control while both of them tried to go for the shank on the ground. Jack delivered multiple knee strikes but Chepe wasn't going down easy. He slipped past Jack and dived for the shank. Jack grabbed his leg and Chepe landed hard against the ground. Jack stood on his leg to hold him down as he reached for the shank but Chepe shouted like a foghorn.

He wasn't able to scream for long before Jack soccer kicked him in the face.

Even then Chepe would cause all the coordinators to

come rushing if he didn't get him to shut up.

Jack made a choice in those few seconds.

Go for the shank or silence him? Jack landed on him and wrapped his hand around his mouth and squeezed his nostrils. Chepe flailed around. It took close to three minutes to suffocate someone, or ten to thirty seconds to choke them. With time against him, he opted to choke him out. He squeezed his forearm hard around his neck, while keeping his other hand over his mouth. Chepe clawed at his arm trying to pry his grip loose but it was useless. Jack was the stronger of the two.

He was nearly unconscious when Jack heard the gate open. His eyes widened but he kept his grip tight. Sure enough, it was the worst thing that could happen. A coordinator stepped into view. He sprang into action, pouncing on Jack.

Jack had no choice but to release Chepe so he could defend himself against the second guy. Chepe rolled and was choking, gasping for air. The coordinator pummeled Jack with his baton while he was still on the ground. Jack grabbed his pant leg and would take his legs out when Noah came into view behind him. His eyes darted from Jack to Chepe, to the coordinator and then before Jack could say another word, he stabbed the coordinator multiple times in the back.

By now Chepe was clawing his way towards the exit on his knees. He had one hand on his throat, and was trying to call out for another coordinator when Jack hauled him back into the darkened enclosure.

Ten more seconds and it was all over. Stabbed, throats slit, Chepe and the coordinator were lying in an ever-increasing puddle of scarlet.

Jack grabbed up the M18 shirt he'd dropped and covered it in blood. While he did that, Noah was acting as a lookout. Once it was done, and the coast was clear they darted out of the cell and made a beeline for the nearest Mara Salvatrucha cell.

Twenty Seven - Riot

There was no surveillance at the prison. It cost too much money and with a government only willing to pay one dollar per person for food each day, they sure as hell wouldn't shell out money on overpriced camera equipment. It would have also meant needing more prison guards on duty and with sixty on payroll and only twelve on shift — it spoke volumes about their priorities.

A lack of surveillance internally and externally was the reason prisoners could get contraband, weapons and other items into the prison. Family, friends and gang members would toss over the wall what they needed. The guards knew it but couldn't stop it. One of the last two riots that Danlí experienced occurred when security guards entered to perform searches for weapons and drugs. There was such a backlash by the inmates that the guards were driven out.

The government wasn't ready to spend unnecessary

money, which meant few eyes would notice Jack and Noah entering or leaving Chepe's cell. And with wives and girlfriends distracting the inmates, they could slip by unnoticed.

When Chepe's body was found by a coordinator, all hell broke loose.

Observing from a place in the courtyard, Jack saw the coordinator rush over to the guards' gate and inform them. A guard crossed from his post to a nearby phone and placed a call. His face was full of concern. Within seconds of getting off the phone he barked orders.

Now it was just a matter of the horse finding the water.

Guards geared up, entered the inner prison and instructed everyone back to their cells. Family members were told to leave. It almost looked like they were wrangling cows by prodding prisoners in the back with batons. No details were provided as to why they were there as they didn't want to incite another riot. And yet by the angry looks they were getting, that's what they were about to get. The coordinators worked with the guards to get everyone to comply. Grumbles permeated the air as inmates demanded to know.

Meanwhile a guard and a coordinator went down to Chepe's cell and disappeared inside. A minute or two later, they emerged. Both of them look concerned not only because they had seen the bodies but because the inmates weren't following instructions.

"We want answers," one said, pushing back on a guard before being knocked to the ground. Word traveled fast inside the compound. Whispers of Chepe's death soon circulated as coordinators tried to maintain control. But it was pointless.

The crowd was riled up and tempers were about to flare.

That's when a Mara Salvatrucha member stepped into view holding the bloody M18 shirt above his head. He was yelling at the top of his voice and attracting all kinds of attention.

A guard elbowed his way through the throng of

worked-up men and snatched it from his hand.

"Where did you find this?"

He pointed to his cell. The guard charged across the courtyard toward Carlos's crew and demanded an answer. Carlos looked at it, then back across at Simón and the others. He turned to his men and asked them if they knew about it. They shrugged and shook their heads.

Carlos turned back and tossed it at the guard.

"They planted that to make it look like it was us. We didn't kill Chepe. Ask why it was in their cell."

That accusation didn't sit well with Simón. Several Mara Salvatrucha gang members pushed their way through the crowd and yelled obscenities. Caught in the middle were the guard and several coordinators. They tried to keep them back but it was pointless.

A bucket filled with piss and shit tissues came soaring overhead and hit one M18 in the face. In that instant, all hell let loose. Men on both sides lunged forward, crashing into each other. Shanks were produced, and blood spilled as violence erupted on a level unseen before even in

Danlí.

Jack tapped Noah on the arm and they squeezed through the crowd of onlookers. Not everyone wanted to get involved. From the tower, several smoke grenades were launched adding to the confusion. Confusion that Jack banked on and planned to use to his advantage.

From outside the prison, the sound of a siren could be heard. It was obvious the guard had made a phone call for backup. For the first time since Jack's arrival, more guards in full riot gear spilled out the back of jeeps and sprinted for the enclosure.

The noise inside the prison was loud as inmates joined in the fight, beating down coordinators and guards alike, while others ran for cover and some took shelter in cells. It was complete pandemonium. Then someone lobbed in the air a Molotov cocktail, it hit the ground and ignited a wooden table. Flames crept up into the air.

Many weapons kept out of sight were produced.

Jack had witnessed only one prison riot in his time in Rikers, and it was quickly subdued by the guards. But this. This was a problem of its own making. Minimal government funding. A prison with a lack of security and surveillance. A warden who didn't give a shit, and inmates who monitored each other. It was all a recipe for disaster.

Someone crashed into Jack as he was making his way towards the north side. He lashed out with a knife and cut him on the arm. Jack retaliated by face palming his nose causing it to burst like a fire hydrant. Jack scooped up the knife and pocketed it.

"Jack!"

He turned to see two men attacking Noah. His eyes darted to a chair nearby. Moving fast, he grabbed it and wielded it like an axe, clobbering one man around the face before diving on him and plunging the knife into his belly.

There was no time for morals.

No time for second-guessing.

Only those who fought back would survive.

Confusion, desperation and anger now dominated Danlí Prison.

More guards flooded into the compound with shields and beat inmates back. Even with sixty guards, and ten or fifteen coordinators, it was no match for the seven hundred strong population. Overcrowding prisons would be their downfall. The air was dense with black and gray smoke as more fires erupted and security from the towers continued to unload smoke grenades.

Jack turned to see Noah twisting a guy's head to one side and then releasing him. For someone who had come from a life without killing, this was his baptism by fire.

They took cover for a few seconds inside the doorway of a cell. Jack's eyes were on the exit where guards were coming in from. A large number remained there trying to keep back the masses while the others fanned out threatening to use sub-machine guns. The strange thing was though they could have used them, they didn't. They were following protocol and the rules for use of power. It was the same in the police. Even though they could carry weapons, they could only use them if they felt their life was in severe jeopardy.

The mass of inmates pushed forward like the tide of the ocean, then they would rush back as rubber bullets were fired at them. Many of them stripped off their tops and threw rocks, chairs, anything they could find.

"Listen up. Follow my lead. Do as I do."

As three guards moved past their cell, Jack darted out and grabbed one of them from behind, he slammed his foot into the back of the guy's knee causing him to buckle. The other two were so preoccupied by the inmates attacking them, they didn't even see their colleague hit the ground. Jack stabbed him in the neck, disabling his ability to fight back and then dragged him back into the cell.

Noah followed suit, though it didn't go as smoothly.

The guard saw him as he rushed at him. He turned and fired a rubber bullet at Noah and he hit the floor. It wouldn't kill him but the pain would take the fight out of him. There was no way he could take the guy down. Jack pulled the handgun from the holster of the man he'd killed and fired a single round into the leg of the guard.

As soon as he went down he rushed out into the horde of prisoners. No one appeared to look on, question or stare. Everyone was too busy either fighting or running for cover.

Jack fired another round into the guard as he reached him and dragged his ass back into the cell. He then returned for Noah. He was coughing from all the smoke. Once inside, he put a drape over the front of the bars and checked on Noah.

"How you holding up?"

"You ever had the wind knocked out of you? Well, multiply that by a hundred. Yeah. I think I can taste breakfast."

Jack snorted. "Give me a hand getting their uniforms off." They stripped the guards and got into their uniforms. Noah was still bent over, clenching his stomach in pain. Jack covered his face with the helmet, goggles and a balaclava that came up over the mouth.

Once ready, they moved out.

"Keep your head down."

Though it was a short distance to the exit, it wasn't easy. Inmates raged, striking them from either side. Jack fired several rounds getting them to clear the way as he hurried Noah through the throng of angry inmates. As they got closer to the exit, he turned his back and kept his head down while firing at the crowd's feet.

He felt a hand grab him from behind and he saw the boot of a fellow guard. The guards shouted in Spanish and pulled both of them back into the safety of the exit. No one was paying attention. No one would. It was fast, furious and out of control.

Supporting Noah, they followed several other injured guards who streamed out of Danlí into the parking lot. More guards arriving on scene hurried to help. Jack broke away from the group climbing into the back of a jeep to be taken for medical attention. As they were crossing the courtyard, heading towards a vehicle, Jack saw the gate open and Lázaro's dark sedan with tinted windows crawl in. It parked in front of the prison and he exited the vehicle, and barked commands to guards.

"Listen up. Wait here, I'll be right back," Jack said.

Noah grabbed him by the arm still wincing in pain.

"Leave it, Jack. Let's go now."

Jack contemplated it for a few seconds, his teeth grinding. He shook his head.

"Stay here."

He placed Noah beside a vehicle and sprinted towards the main entrance with gun in hand. He didn't have to worry about anyone recognizing him as he was dressed in dark security guard fatigues, the lower half of his face was covered by a black balaclava and the top half with goggles and a riot helmet. While not all wore the balaclava, others did for several reasons. Some security guards didn't want known gang members to target their families beyond the prison. It gave them some sense of privacy and security.

Lázaro was telling guards to get in there and use whatever force was required to subdue the inmates. He turned and looked at Jack for a second but it was only to tell him and another guard to go with him up to the tower.

Jack fell in line. The one guard was ahead while Jack remained behind Lázaro. On the way to the tower, Lázaro was spitting orders out over the radio. A guard inside communicated that they were losing control and eight guards were already confirmed dead. The body count of prisoners was even higher.

"Fuck!"

As they ascended the spiral steps, Jack looked back to see if any other guards were following. Over the side of the steel bannister was a long drop to the ground. Their boots pounded the worn stone staircase that took them up to the first guard tower. Once they reached the top there was only one other guard. Lázaro turned and grabbed a hold of Jack and pushed him towards the front, telling him to open fire upon anyone who was killing the guards.

Meanwhile, Lázaro raised a megaphone speaker and shouted for the inmates to listen, but his words fell on deaf ears. They were done with listening. In the heat of a riot no one cared about anyone's commands, especially the warden's.

Jack fired off a few rounds into the crowd, making sure not to hit anyone. Out the corner of his eye he saw Lázaro set the radio down to continue his rant over the megaphone. Jack shifted position and fired a few more rounds, then scooped up the radio and dropped it over the edge. The last thing he needed was more guards making their way up.

He then stepped back and fired two rounds into the heads of security. Their bodies dropped hard and Lázaro spun around to find Jack holding a handgun to his head. Total shock lit up his face as Jack pulled down the balaclava covering his mouth and lifted his visor.

"Put the megaphone on the ground."

Lázaro dropped it. It let out this high-pitched sound then stopped.

"Get on your knees."

"You won't get away with this."

"I already have. Now get on your knees."

Jack's eyes darted back and forth between Lázaro and

the riot that wasn't even close to being over. Attached to the wall was a fire axe, and a fire hose. Keeping his gun on him, he pulled at the hose until it unrolled from the housing.

A split second of taking his eyes off Lázaro was all that was required.

Lázaro withdrew a small pistol he must have had in a holster attached to his lower leg. It happened so fast. He unloaded a round into Jack knocking him back. It struck him in the body armor. There was a flash in his peripheral vision as Lázaro shot towards the door and started his descent. Jack could hear him panting hard, his boots pounding the stone. Jack groaned as he rose to his feet, grabbed the end of the fire hose, rushed towards the door and jumped over the edge in between the staircase with little thought to how long the hose went. His body dropped fast, the fire hose letting out a wheeling sound until it went out about halfway down. He jerked up for a second, then slammed into the side.

He groaned. "Gonna feel that tomorrow," he muttered

and climbed over and started his ascent to head him off. Lázaro leaned over and fired several slugs. Chunks of stone spat as Jack continued up, keeping the Glock in his hand out in front of him.

It was a race to the top of the guardhouse. Jack knew the second he got up there he would scream for help from that megaphone. His thighs burned with every two steps he took. Lázaro fired multiple times but Jack stayed out of view and kept moving forward.

As Jack burst out onto the top of the guardhouse. Lázaro already had the megaphone in one hand, and the small gun in the other.

"Too late."

Lázaro squeezed the trigger but it clicked in his hand.

The magazine was empty.

He inhaled to scream and part of it came out but was quickly cut short as Jack fired a round into his knee. Lázaro collapsed on the ground, the megaphone slid towards Jack. He kicked it out of the way, fired another round into Lázaro's second knee. He then crouched down beside him.

"You were saying," Jack said with a smirk.

"Please. Please."

He begged for his life. Tears streaming down his face, as he coughed and groaned in agony. Jack looked over his body. His knees were messed up.

"Where's my money?"

"And you'll let me live?"

"Where is it?"

"At my house, in the office. There is a safe located inside my desk. The combination is 453189. Now please. Please don't kill me."

"Oh shut the hell up."

Jack got up and headed over to the entrance. A south wind blew in, kicking up dust and grit. He pulled up his balaclava to hide his face. Over the side the riot continued, though now the inmates appeared to be fighting more with themselves than the few remaining guards.

"Thank you," Lázaro said in his most pitiful voice. It

never ceased to amaze Jack how quickly a man could change his tune when faced with imminent death.

"For what?" Jack asked before stepping out and pulling up the fire hose.

He could hear Lázaro saying something but he wasn't paying any attention. Once he had reeled in the hose he returned and tied it around Lázaro's neck.

"What the hell? You said you wouldn't kill me."

"I didn't say that."

"But... But..."

Jack grabbed his face and looked directly into his eyes.

"Did you know it takes very little strength to stop a man's breathing if you know where to apply pressure?"

He tossed Lázaro's own words back at him.

"Please. No."

"Keys to your car."

"I..."

Jack snapped his fingers in front of his face. "Keys!"

He fished around in his pocket and pulled out a set. Jack checked the rest of his pockets.

Jack then crouched down, and hauled his body up. Lázaro yelled but his cries were lost in the chaos taking place below. He tried to cling to him but Jack pried loose his feeble grip and tossed him over the side of the wall down into the compound. He didn't stick around to see what happened. He heard it as he made his way down. He knew he was dead when silence fell over the prison. They were looking, staring at the man that had caused so many deaths and had robbed them of what small rights they had.

Once on the ground, Jack rushed back to the parking lot.

"Jack."

"Time to get out of here."

He hauled Noah up and carried him over to Lázaro's vehicle.

They slipped inside, he turned over the ignition and drove out the open gate.

* * *

After retrieving the money, along with an extra

hundred grand to make up for the trouble, Jack made one final visit before heading north to the border.

José, the man that was meant to use his power to help those inside, was watching the riot unfold on television from the comfort of his office. Like many others, he abused his place of authority. No words were exchanged when Jack walked into the room and fired upon him. He didn't even give him a chance to open his mouth.

He'd heard enough pleading for one day.

Blood sprayed across the TV set.

His body slumped to the floor.

The execution was cold.

But justified.

Twenty Eight - Road Home

Jack and Noah drove out of the city and headed north into Guatemala after ditching the vehicle and uniforms. They paid a man to take them over the border and then slowly made their way north. The only upside to being on the run in a country that was corrupt was everyone had a price to remain silent.

That's where that extra hundred grand came in handy.

Without passports, they couldn't fly but they didn't seem to mind. It gave them a chance to get to know each other. They stayed in several good hotels, ate well and at the first chance they got, Noah called home.

Liz was beyond relieved.

Jack chewed away on beef jerky as they stayed a night in a hotel somewhere in the middle of Hermosillo, Mexico. The TV was playing, as Noah made a phone call. Reports on the riot had made headlines. Mostly for the number of deaths but also because word of the conditions had spread to human rights advocates. They were now calling for a complete revamp of prison policy in light of allegations made against Lázaro.

The same crooked law officials that had assisted Lázaro in the beginning would sweep most of what had occurred under the rug. Atrocious conditions in Honduras prisons would continue until someone changed them. Until then, their cry for justice would fade into the background.

The upside was no more men would be forced to fight to the death to line the pockets of a greedy warden. There was no mention of Jack and Noah's escape or Henry's death, which was no surprise. Still, he'd checked online at a local Internet café every few days for news reports. Nothing. He assumed that among the underhanded dealings that Lázaro had made, some of them included the arrest and incarceration of innocent men. It was easier to make the innocent disappear than to explain why they had died in prison.

No doubt, those who had got into bed with him had some kind of exit plan in place that would allow them to wash their hands of any involvement.

Noah hung up and lay on his bed. He tossed a few peanuts in his mouth.

"How is she?" Jack asked.

"Unable to wait." He paused. "What are you going to do when we get back to the USA?"

Jack shrugged, rubbed his eye and took a swig of his beer.

"Why don't you stick around a while?"

"That doesn't tend to work well for me."

There was silence between them, only the drone of a news anchor rambling on about the current state of Honduras before shifting gears to the latest lotto numbers.

"Jack. You know I appreciate what you did for me."

"Don't worry about it."

"No, I mean it, I wouldn't have survived in there much longer."

"Maybe. You'd be surprised how quickly we adapt to our surroundings."

Noah opened his mouth to say something then gazed down.

"What you did back there, with those guards. You didn't hesitate to kill."

"And?"

"In the cage I can understand it, even outside being attacked in a riot. We had no choice. But…"

"You're out, that's all that matters."

Jack rose from his seat and went over to the window and looked out. It had become habit. Though he was pretty certain that no one would come looking, especially not in Mexico, he still did it. In the reflection of the window he saw Noah reach for his beer before he continued to pepper Jack with questions.

"Was dad, I mean, was Eddie part of the Mafia?"

Jack snorted. "Eddie? No. He warned me against them." He sighed. "I didn't listen. Too young, too cocky. I thought I knew best."

"How did he die?"

Jack hesitated before he replied. Painful memories

flooded in. "Trying to protect our sister."

Noah nodded, and placed his beer on a side table before heading into the bathroom. He stood at the door for a second as if another question was weighing on his mind.

"Will you ever return to New York?" Noah asked.

Had he been asked that ten years ago, he would have laughed. New York had been home for so long. Back then had no reason to venture out, but now… the Big Apple only held bad memories.

"Perhaps one day."

* * *

Three days later, Liz was there to greet them as they arrived at her home. Jack watched as she hugged Noah and wept on his shoulder. Jack stood by the car feeling as though he was peering into a moment he knew nothing about — like a missing piece of a jigsaw puzzle. He knew something was missing from his life but he'd lived so long without it, it no longer mattered.

His mother didn't greet him the same, and yet he

never expected her to.

"Thank you, Jack."

She reached out and shook his hand. As she did it, she pulled him in for a hug. It was an awkward exchange, clumsy, unnatural even. His only memory of her had been from an old photo. And yet here she was trying to bridge the gap of forty years. She stepped back.

Noah walked back to her and put his arm around her and squeezed.

"Well, come on in," she said turning to head back into the house.

"Actually, I think I'll be going."

"But you just got here," Noah said, frowning.

He pushed off the banged-up, ten-year-old vehicle they'd picked up from some used car lot in Tucson. He smiled. "I should keep moving."

"You have a restless heart," his mother said.

He shrugged. Jack tossed the keys to Noah. "Keep it."

He chuckled. "As if. The damn thing broke down on us twice."

Liz stepped forward. "Jack, you don't need to go. At least stay for supper."

He looked off down the long stretch of road with palm trees either side. He had nowhere in particular to go. No pressing matter. He'd always wondered what his mother would have been like, and what he would do if he'd had the chance to know her. Now it was before him, he felt like a fish out of water. As the ocean waves crashed against the shore, and a fading sun waned behind the trees, he looked back at the two of them.

He squinted, and cupped a hand to block the glare. "Okay, but just for a meal."

Noah smirked, moved in fast and wrapped his arm around Jack's neck. On the way in, Noah continued to rattle on and Jack just smiled. "You know, Jack, I thought we could go into business. I have this great idea for a new importing and exporting venture."

As his mother held the door open, Jack caught her eye.

In that split second, he realized several things.

She might not have been the mother he had imagined.

Nor could he fully grasp her reasons for leaving so many years ago.

But in that moment, he was no longer a drifter, an ex-hit man, or a stranger with no fixed abode, he was a son, a brother, a friend, with a place he could call home — if only for an evening.

* * *

THANK YOU FOR READING

Hard Time: Debt Collector: Book #8

Sign up at www.jonmills.com for news on new releases.

NEWSLETTER

Thank you for buying Debt Collector 8: Hard Time

Building a relationship with readers is one of the best things about writing. I occasionally send out a newsletter with details on new releases and subscriber only special offers. For instance, with each new release of a book, you will be alerted to it at a subscriber only discounted rate.

Go here to receive special offers, bonus content, and news about Jon's new books, sign up for the newsletter. http://www.jonmills.com/

A PLEA...

If you enjoyed the book, I would really appreciate it if you would consider leaving a review. I can't stress how helpful this is in helping other readers decide if they should give it a shot. Reviews from readers like you are the best recommendation a book can have. Without reviews, an author's books are virtually invisible on the retail sites. It also lets me know what you liked. You can leave a review by visiting the book's page. I would greatly appreciate it. It only takes a couple of seconds.

Thank you — **Jon Mills**

JON MILLS

Jon Mills is originally from England. He currently lives in Ontario, Canada with his family. He is the author of The Debt Collector series, The Promise, True Connection, Lost Girls (Out 2017) and the Undisclosed Trilogy. To get more information about upcoming books or if you wish to get in touch with Jon, you can do so using the following contact information:

Twitter: Jon_Mills

Facebook: authorjonmills

Website: www.jonmills.com

Email: contact@jonmills.com

Made in the USA
Lexington, KY
03 March 2019